The Houseguest

Amparo Dávila

THE
HOUSEGUEST

and other stories

*Translated from the Spanish
by Audrey Harris & Matthew Gleeson*

A NEW DIRECTIONS PAPERBOOK ORIGINAL

The stories included in this volume were selected from Amparo Dávila's *Cuentos reunidos*, published by Fondo de Cultura Económica (2009).

"Moses and Gaspar" was first published in English by the *Paris Review*.

First published as a New Directions Paperbook Original (NDP1428) in 2018
Manufactured in the United States of America

Library of Congress Cataloging-in-Publication Data
Dávila, Amparo, author. | Harris, Audrey, 1981– translator. |
Gleeson, Matthew, translator.
Title: The houseguest and other stories / by Amparo Dávila ;
translated from the Spanish by Audrey Harris and Matthew Gleeson.
Description: New York : New Directions, 2018.
Identifiers: LCCN 2018021513 (print) | LCCN 2018024713 (ebook) |
ISBN 9780811228220 (ebook) | ISBN 9780811228213 (acid-free paper)
Classification: LCC PQ7297.D315 (ebook) | LCC PQ7297.D315 A2 2018 (print) |
DDC 863/.64—dc22
LC record available at https://lccn.loc.gov/2018021513

20 19 18 17 16 15 14 13 12

New Directions Books are published for James Laughlin
by New Directions Publishing Corporation
80 Eighth Avenue, New York 10011

Contents

The Houseguest

Moses and Gaspar

THE TRAIN ARRIVED at about six o'clock on a cold, wet November morning. The fog was so thick it was almost impossible to see. I was wearing my coat collar up and my hat shoved down around my ears, but still the fog penetrated all the way to my bones. Leonidas lived in a neighborhood far from the center of town, on the sixth floor of a modest apartment building. Everything—the staircase, the hallways, the rooms—was invaded by the fog. As I climbed the stairs I thought I was approaching eternity, an eternity of mist and silence. Leonidas, my brother, when I reached your door, I thought I would die of grief! I had come to visit you the year before, during my Christmas break. "We'll have turkey stuffed with olives and chestnuts, an Italian Spumante, and dried fruit," you said, radiant with happiness, "Moses, Gaspar, let's celebrate!" Those days were always so festive. We drank a lot and talked about our parents, about the apple *pasteles*, the evenings by the fire, the old man's pipe and his absent, downcast gaze that we couldn't forget, the winter sweaters that Mamá knitted for us, that aunt on our mother's side who buried all her money and died of hunger, the professor of mathematics with his starched collars and bow ties, the girls from the drugstore we took to the movies on Sundays, those films we never watched, the handkerchiefs covered in lipstick that we had to throw away ... In my grief, I had forgotten to ask the concierge to unlock the apartment. I had to wake her up; she climbed the stairs half asleep, dragging her feet. There were Moses and Gaspar, but when they saw me they fled in terror. The woman said she'd been feeding them twice a day—and yet, to me, they looked all skin and bones.

"It was horrible, Señor Kraus. I saw him with my own eyes, here in this chair, slumped over the table. Moses and Gaspar were lying at his feet. At first I thought they were all asleep—they were so quiet! But it was already late and Señor Leonidas would always wake up early and go out to buy food for Moses and Gaspar. He ate downtown, but he always fed them first; I suddenly realized that ..."

I made some coffee and tried to pull myself together before going to the funeral parlor. Leonidas, Leonidas, how could it be? Leonidas, so full of life, how could you be lying stiff in a cold refrigerator drawer?...

The funeral was at four in the afternoon. It was raining and the cold was intense; everything was gray, with only black hats and umbrellas interrupting the monotony; raincoats and faces blurred into the fog and drizzle. A fair number of people had come to the funeral: coworkers, perhaps, and a few friends. I navigated within the bitterest of dreams. I wanted this day to be over, to wake up without that knot in my throat, without the mind-numbing sense of being torn apart. An old priest said a prayer and blessed the grave. Afterward, someone I didn't recognize handed me a cigarette and took me by the arm in a familiar way, offering his condolences. We left the cemetery; Leonidas stayed behind, forever.

I walked alone, aimless, beneath the persistent, dull rain. Hopeless, crippled in my soul. My only happiness, the one great affection that tied me to this earth, had died with

4

Leonidas. We had been inseparable since childhood, but for years the war kept us apart. Finding each other again, after the fighting and the solitude, was the greatest joy of our lives. We were the only two left in the family: nevertheless, we soon realized that we ought to live separate lives, and that's what we did. During those years, each of us had acquired his own customs, habits, and absolute independence. Leonidas found a job as a bank teller; I went to work for an insurance company as an accountant. During the week, both of us dedicated ourselves to our own work or solitude; but Sundays we always spent together. How happy we were then! I assure you, we both looked forward to that day of the week.

Sometime later they moved Leonidas to another city. He could have quit and looked for another position. His way, though, was always to accept things with exemplary serenity. "It's useless to resist; we could circle around a thousand times and always end up where we began ..." "We've been so happy, there had to be a catch; happiness comes at a price ..." This was his philosophy and he bore it calmly and without defiance. "There are some things you can't fight against, my dear José ..."

Leonidas went away. For a time, his absence was more than I could bear; then slowly we began to organize our solitary lives. We wrote to each other once or twice a month. I spent my vacations with him and he came to see me during his. And so our lives went by ...

Night had fallen by the time I returned to his apartment. The cold was more intense and it was still raining. I had a bottle of rum under my arm, which I'd bought from a store that I'd found open. The apartment was utterly dark and freezing. I stumbled my way in, switched on the light, and connected the heater. I uncorked the bottle nervously, with clumsy, trembling hands. There, at the table, in the last spot that Leonidas had occupied, I sat down to drink, to vent my sorrow. At least I was alone and didn't have to hold back or hide my pain from anyone; I could weep and cry and ... Suddenly I felt eyes behind me. I jumped out of the chair and spun around: there were Moses and Gaspar. I had forgotten all about them, but there they were, staring at me—with hostility? With mistrust? I couldn't tell. But their gaze was terrible. In the moment I didn't know what to tell them. I felt hollowed out and absent, as though I were outside myself and had lost the power to think. Besides, I didn't know how much they understood ... I went on drinking ... Then I realized that they were both silently weeping. The tears dripped from their eyes and fell to the floor; they wept with no expression and without a sound. At around midnight, I made coffee and prepared them a bit of food. They wouldn't touch it, only went on crying disconsolately ...

Leonidas had arranged all of his affairs. Perhaps he had burned his files, because I didn't find a single one in the apartment. As far as I knew, he'd sold his furniture on the pretext that he was going away; it was all going to be picked up the next day. His clothes and other personal effects were carefully packed in two trunks labeled with my name. His savings and the money from the furniture had been deposited in the bank, also in my name. Everything was in order. The only things he left me in charge of were his burial and the care of Moses and Gaspar.

At around four in the morning we departed for the train station: our train left at five fifteen. Moses and Gaspar had to travel, to their obvious disgust, in the baggage car; they weren't allowed to ride with the passengers—not at any price. What a grueling trip! I was physically and morally spent. I'd gone four days and four nights without sleeping or resting, ever since the telegram had arrived with the news that Leonidas was dead. I tried to sleep during the trip but only managed to doze. In the stations where the train made longer stops, I went to check on Moses and Gaspar and see if they wanted something to eat. The sight of them wounded me. They seemed to be recriminating me for their situation. "You know it's not my fault," I repeated each time, but they couldn't, or didn't want to, understand. It was going to be very difficult for me to live with them: they'd never taken to me, and I felt uncomfortable in their presence, as though I were always being watched. How unpleasant it had been to find them in his house that past summer! Leonidas evaded my questions and begged me in the warmest terms to love them and put up with them. "The poor things deserve to be loved," he told me. That vacation was exhausting and violent, even though the mere fact of seeing Leonidas filled me with happiness. He had stopped coming to visit me, since he couldn't leave Moses and Gaspar alone. The next year—the last time I saw Leonidas—everything went more normally. I didn't like Moses and Gaspar and I never would, but they no longer made me so uneasy. I never found out how they came to live with Leonidas ... Now they were with me, a legacy, an inheritance from my unforgettable brother.

It was after eleven at night when we arrived at my house. The train had been delayed more than four hours. The three of us were completely worn out. All that I had to offer Moses and Gaspar was some fruit and a little bit of cheese. They ate without enthusiasm, watching me suspiciously. I threw some blankets down in the living room so they could sleep, then shut myself in my room and took a sleeping pill.

The next day was Sunday, which meant I was spared from having to go to work—not that I could have gone. I had planned to sleep late, but I began to hear noises at the first light of dawn. It was Moses and Gaspar: they had already woken up and were pacing from one side of the apartment to the other. They came up to my bedroom door and stood there, pressing themselves against it, as if they were trying to see through the keyhole, or maybe just listening for the sound of my breathing to see whether I was still asleep. Then I remembered that Leonidas fed them every morning at seven. I had to get up and find them something to eat.

What hard and arduous days those were after Moses and Gaspar came to live in my house! I was used to waking up a little before eight, making coffee, and leaving for the office at eight thirty, since the bus took half an hour and my job started at nine. With Moses and Gaspar there, my whole life was thrown into chaos. I had to wake up at six to buy milk and other groceries, then make their breakfast—they ate punctually at seven, according to their habit. If I was late, they grew furious, which frightened me because I didn't know just how far their anger might go. I had to clean up the apartment every day, because with them there, I always found everything out of place.

But what tortured me the most was their hopeless grief. The way they searched for Leonidas and stood waiting for him at the door. Sometimes, when I came home from work, they ran jubilantly to greet me, but as soon as they saw it was me, they put on such disappointed, suffering faces that I broke down and wept along with them. This was the only thing we shared. There were days when they hardly got up; they spent all day lying there, listless, taking no interest in anything. I would have liked to know what they were thinking then. The fact was that I hadn't explained anything to them when I went to pick them up. I don't know if Leonidas had said something to them, or if they knew ...

Moses and Gaspar had been living with me for almost a month when I finally realized the serious problem they were going to create in my life. For several years I'd had a romantic

8

relationship with the cashier of a restaurant where I often ate. Our friendship began in a straightforward way, because I've never been the courting kind. I simply needed a woman, and Susy solved that problem. At first, we only saw each other now and then. Sometimes a month or two would pass in which we did nothing more than greet each other at the restaurant with a nod of the head, like mere acquaintances. I would go on living calmly for a while, without thinking about her, then all at once I'd feel old and familiar symptoms of anxiety, sudden rages, and melancholy. Then I'd look up Susy and everything would return to normal. After a while, almost habitually, Susy came to visit once a week. When I went to pay the check for dinner, I'd say, "Tonight, Susy." If she was free—since she did have other engagements—she'd answer, "I'll see you tonight," otherwise it was, "Not tonight, but tomorrow if you like." Susy's other engagements didn't bother me; we owed each other nothing and didn't belong to each other. Advancing in years and abundant in flesh, she was far from being a beauty; but she smelled good and always wore silk underwear with lace trim, which had a notable influence on my desire. I've never managed to recall even one of her dresses, but her intimate combinations I remember well. We never spoke while making love; instead, the two of us both seemed lost inside ourselves. When we said goodbye, I always gave her some money. "You're very generous," she would say in satisfaction; but beyond this customary gift, she never asked me for anything. The death of Leonidas interrupted our routine relations. More than a month passed before I went looking for Susy. I'd spent the whole month in the most hopeless grief, which I shared with no one but Moses and Gaspar, who were just as much strangers to me as I was to them. Finally one night I waited for Susy at the corner outside the restaurant, as usual, and we went up to my apartment. Everything happened so quickly that I was only able to

9

piece it together afterward. When Susy entered the bedroom, she saw Moses and Gaspar there, cornered in fright under the sofa. She turned so pale that I thought she was going to faint, then she screamed like a lunatic and dashed down the stairs. I ran after her and had a hard time calming her down. After that unfortunate accident, Susy never came back to my apartment. When I wanted to see her, I had to rent a hotel room, which threw off my budget and annoyed me.

The incident with Susy was only the first in a series of calamities.

"Señor Kraus," the concierge said to me one day, "all of the tenants have come to complain about the unbearable noise that comes from your apartment as soon as you leave for the office. Please do something about it, because there are people like Señorita X or Señor A who work at night and need to sleep during the day."

I was taken aback and didn't know what to think. Overwhelmed as they were by the loss of their owner, Moses and Gaspar lived in silence. At least that's how they were when I was in the apartment. Seeing them so downcast and diminished, I said nothing—it seemed too cruel. Besides, I had no evidence against them ...

"I'm sorry to bother you again, but this can't go on," the concierge told me a few days later. "As soon as you leave, they start dumping all the stuff in the kitchen on the floor, they throw the chairs around, they move the beds and all the furniture. And the screams, the screams, Señor Kraus, are horrible; we can't take it anymore, and it lasts all day until you come home."

I decided to investigate. I asked permission at the office to take a few hours off. I came home at noon. The concierge and all the tenants were right. The whole building seemed about to collapse with the unbearable racket that was coming from my apartment. I opened the door. Moses was on top of the stove, bombarding Gaspar from above with pots and pans, while Gaspar ran around dodging the projectiles, screaming and laughing like a maniac. They were so engaged in their game that they didn't notice me there. The chairs were overturned, the pillows flung onto the table, onto the floor ... When they saw me, they froze.

"I can't believe what I'm seeing!" I shouted in rage. "I've gotten complaints from all the neighbors and I refused to believe them. How ungrateful! This is how you repay my hospitality and honor your master's memory? His death is ancient history to you, it happened so long ago you don't even feel it—all you care about are your games. You little demons, you ingrates!"

When I finished, I realized they were lying on the floor in tears. I left them there and returned to the office. I felt bad all the rest of the day. When I came home in the afternoon, the house had been cleaned up and they were hiding in the closet. I felt terrible pangs of remorse; I felt that I'd been too hard on those poor creatures. Maybe, I thought, they don't know that Leonidas is never coming back, maybe they think that he's only gone on a trip and that one day he'll return—maybe the more they hope, the less it hurts. And I've destroyed the only thing that makes them happy ... But my remorse ended soon enough; the next day I learned that they had been at it again: the noise, the screams ...

Not long after this I was evicted by court order, and so we began moving from place to place. A month here, another there, another there ... One night, I was feeling worn down and depressed by the series of disasters that had befallen me. We had a small apartment consisting of a tiny living room, a kitchen, a bathroom, and one bedroom. I decided to turn in for the night. When I went into the bedroom, I saw that they were asleep on my bed. Then I remembered: the last time I'd visited Leonidas, on the night I arrived, I noticed that my brother was improvising two beds in the living room. "Moses and Gaspar sleep in the bedroom, we'll have to make ourselves comfortable out here," he said, rather self-consciously. At the time, I couldn't understand how Leonidas could possibly bend to the will of those two miserable creatures. Now I understood ... From that day on, they occupied my bed and there was nothing I could do about it.

I had never been close with my neighbors, because I found the idea exhausting. I preferred my solitude, my independence. Still, we greeted each other on the stairs, in the hallways, in the street ... With the arrival of Moses and Gaspar, all of that changed. In every apartment we stayed in—which was never for very long—the neighbors developed a fierce hatred for me. There always came a point when I became afraid to enter the building or to leave my apartment. Returning home late at night, after having been with Susy, I thought I might be assaulted. I heard doors opening as I went by, or footsteps behind me, furtive, silent, someone's breath ... When I finally entered my apartment I would be bathed in cold sweat and trembling from head to toe.

Soon I had to give up my job; I was afraid that if I left them alone, they might be killed. There was such hatred in everyone's eyes! It would have been easy to break into the apartment; or the concierge might even have opened it himself, because he hated them, too. I quit my job, and my only source of income was the bookkeeping I could do at home, small accounts that weren't enough to live on. I left early in the morning, when it was still dark, to buy the food I cooked myself. I didn't go out again except to turn in or pick up the ledgers, and I did this as fast as I could, almost running, so that I wouldn't be out long. I stopped seeing Susy; I no longer had the time or the money. I couldn't leave them alone, either by day or by night, and she refused ever to come back to my apartment. Bit by bit I began to run through my savings, and then through the money Leonidas had left me. I was earning a pittance, not even enough for food, much less the constant moving from place to place. So I decided to go away.

With the money I had left, I bought a small old farm outside the city and a few essential pieces of furniture. It's an isolated house, half in ruins. There the three of us will live, far from everything but safe from ambush and assault, tightly joined by an invisible bond, by a stark, cold hatred and an indecipherable design.

Everything is ready for our departure—everything, or rather, the little there is to bring with us. Moses and Gaspar are also awaiting the moment when we will set off. I can tell by their air of anxiety. I think they're satisfied. Their eyes shine. If only I could know what they're thinking! But no, I would be afraid to plumb the shadowy mystery of their being. Silently they approach me, as if they wanted to sniff out my mood or, perhaps, to find out what I'm thinking. But I know they can sense it, they must, for it shows in their joy, in the air of triumph that fills them whenever I feel a longing to destroy them. And they know I can't, they know I'll never fulfill my most ardent desire. They enjoy it ... How many times would I have killed them if it had been up to me! Leonidas, Leonidas, I can't even judge your decision! You loved me, no doubt, as I loved you, but your death and your legacy have destroyed my life. I don't want to think or believe that you coldly condemned me or planned my ruin. No, I know it is something stronger than we are. I don't blame you, Leonidas: even if this is your doing, it was meant to be: "We could have circled around a thousand times and always ended up where we began."

The Houseguest

I'LL NEVER FORGET the day he came to live with us. My husband brought him home from a trip.

At the time we'd been married for almost three years, we had two children, and I wasn't happy. My husband thought of me as something like a piece of furniture, one that you're used to seeing in a particular spot but that doesn't make the slightest impression. We lived in a small, isolated town, far from the city. A town that was almost dead, or about to disappear.

I couldn't suppress a cry of horror the first time I saw him. He was grim, sinister, with large yellowish eyes, unblinking and almost circular, that seemed to pierce through things and people.

My already miserable life became hell. The very night he arrived, I begged my husband not to condemn me to the torture of his company. I couldn't help it: he filled me with mistrust and horror. "He's completely inoffensive," my husband said, looking at me with marked indifference. "You'll get used to having him around, and if you don't ..." It was impossible to convince my husband to take him away. He stayed in our house.

I wasn't the only one who suffered because of his presence. Everyone in the house—my children, the woman who helped me with the chores, her little son—they all dreaded him. Only my husband enjoyed having him around.

From the first day, my husband gave him the corner room. It was a large room, but I never used it because it was dark and damp. He, however, seemed content in there. Being quite dark, it suited his needs. He would sleep until night fell; I never discovered what time he went to bed.

I lost what little peace I had enjoyed in that big house. During the day, everything seemed to proceed normally. I always rose very early, dressed the children—who would already be awake—gave them breakfast, and entertained them while Guadalupe fixed up the house and went out to do the shopping.

The house was very large, with a garden in the middle and the rooms laid out around it. Between the rooms and the garden there were corridors that protected the rooms from the harshness of the frequent rains and wind. Caring for such a large house and its garden—my morning activity each day—was hard work. But I loved my garden. The passageways were covered with climbing plants that flowered almost all year round. I remember how much I enjoyed sitting in one of those corridors during the afternoon, sewing the children's clothes amid the perfume of the honeysuckle and the bougainvillea.

In the garden I grew chrysanthemums, pansies, Alpine violets, begonias, and heliotropes. While I watered the plants, the children entertained themselves looking for caterpillars among the leaves. Sometimes they would spend hours, silent and very intent, trying to catch the drops of water that leaked from the old garden hose.

I couldn't keep myself from glancing now and then toward the corner room. Although he spent all day sleeping, I couldn't be sure. There were times when, as I was cooking in the afternoon, I suddenly saw his shadow cast upon the wood stove. I would feel him behind me ... I'd throw down whatever I was holding and run from the kitchen screaming like a madwoman. He would go back to his room, as if nothing had happened.

I think he was completely unaware of Guadalupe; he never approached her or chased after her. Not so with me and the children. He hated them, and he stalked me constantly.

When he left his room, there began the most terrible nightmare a person could endure. He always stationed himself under a small arbor in front of my bedroom door. I stopped leaving my bedroom. Several times, thinking he was still asleep, I would head toward the kitchen to make the children a snack, then suddenly discover him in some dark corner of the walkway, beneath the flowering vines. "He's there already, Guadalupe!" I would shout desperately.

Guadalupe and I never referred to him by name. It seemed to us that doing so would lend greater reality to that shadowy being. We always said, "There he is, he's come out, he's sleeping—he, he, he ..."

He only took two meals, one when he woke up at dusk and the other, perhaps, in the early morning before he went to sleep. Guadalupe was responsible for bringing him the tray; I can assure you that she flung it into his room, for the poor woman was just as terrified as I was. He ate nothing but meat; he wouldn't touch anything else.

After the children had gone to sleep, Guadalupe would bring dinner to my room. I couldn't leave them alone, knowing that he had gotten up or was about to. Once her chores were finished, Guadalupe went off to bed with her little boy, leaving me alone to watch over my children's slumber. As my bedroom door was always left unlocked, I didn't dare go to sleep, fearing that he could come in and attack us at any moment. And it wasn't possible to lock the door; my husband always came home late, and if he found it locked, he would have thought ... And he came home very late. He had a lot of work, he said once. I think other things kept him entertained as well ...

One night I was awake until almost two in the morning, hearing him outside ... When I woke up, I saw him next to my bed, staring at me with his piercing gaze ... I leaped out of bed and threw the gasoline lamp at him, the one I left burning all night. There was no electricity in that town, and I couldn't have endured the darkness, knowing that at any moment ... He dodged the lamp and left the room; it shattered on the brick floor and the gasoline quickly burst into flame. If it hadn't been for Guadalupe, who came running when I screamed, the whole house would have burned down.

My husband had no time to listen to me, nor did he care what happened in the house. We only spoke when absolutely necessary. We had long since run out of words and affection.

I feel sick all over again when I remember ... Guadalupe had gone out shopping and left her little Martín sleeping in a crate where she used to lay him down during the day. I checked on him several times; he was sleeping peacefully. It was almost noon. I was combing my children's hair when I heard the little boy's crying mingled with strange shouts. I reached the room and found him cruelly beating the boy. I still can't explain how I wrested the little child from his grasp and hurled myself at him with a heavy stick I found at hand, attacking him with all the fury I'd kept pent up for so long. I don't know if I managed to hurt him much, because I fell down in a faint. When Guadalupe came back from her shopping, she found me unconscious and her little boy covered with bruises and bloody scratches. Her pain and rage were terrible. Fortunately the boy didn't die and he soon recovered.

I was afraid that Guadalupe would run away and leave me alone with him. If she didn't, it was because she was a brave and noble woman who felt great affection for my children and for me. But that day a hatred was born in her that clamored for vengeance.

I told my husband what had happened and demanded that he be sent away, pleading that he could kill our children the way he had tried to do with little Martín. "Every day you're more hysterical, it's truly painful and depressing to see you like this … I've explained to you a thousand times that he's harmless."

I thought then about fleeing from that house, from my husband, from him … But I had no money and no easy way to communicate with anyone. Without friends or family to turn to, I felt as alone as an orphan.

My children were terrified; they didn't want to play in the garden anymore—they wouldn't leave my side. Whenever Guadalupe went out to the market, I shut myself in my room with them.

"This situation can't go on," I said to Guadalupe one day.

"We have to do something, and soon," she replied.

"But what can the two of us do alone?"

"Alone, true, but with such hatred …"

Her eyes held a strange gleam. I felt afraid and overjoyed.

The opportunity arrived when we least expected it. My husband left for the city to take care of some business. He would be away for a while, he told me, some twenty days.

I don't know if he was aware that my husband was gone, but that day he woke up earlier than usual and stationed himself in front of my room. Guadalupe and her son slept in my room, and for the first time I could lock the door.

Guadalupe and I spent almost the entire night making plans. The children slept peacefully. From time to time we heard him come up to the door of the room and pound on it furiously ...

The next day we gave the three children their breakfast and then, so that we could work calmly without them interfering with our plans, we shut them in my room. Guadalupe and I had so much to do and were in such a hurry to do it that we couldn't spare time even to eat.

Guadalupe sawed several large, sturdy planks while I looked for a hammer and nails. When everything was ready, we silently crept toward the corner room. The double door was ajar. Holding our breath, we closed the door, dropped the bolt, then locked it and began to nail the planks across it until we had completely sealed it shut. Thick drops of sweat ran down our foreheads as we worked. He didn't make any noise; he was seemingly fast asleep. When it was all finished, Guadalupe and I hugged each other, crying.

The following days were awful. He lived for a long time without air, without light, without food ... At first he pounded at the door, throwing himself against it; he shouted desperately, clawed and scratched ... Neither Guadalupe nor I could eat or sleep—his screams were terrible! Sometimes we thought my husband would come back before he was dead. If he were to find him that way! ... His endurance was great; I think he lasted nearly two weeks ...

One day there was nothing to be heard. No more noises, not even a moan ... Still, we waited two more days before opening the room.

When my husband returned, we greeted him with the news of his guest's sudden and disconcerting death.

Fragment of a Diary
[July and August]

Monday, July 7

My neighbor Señor Rojas seemed surprised to find me sitting on the stairs. Surely what drew his attention was my gaze, conspicuously sad. I noticed the vivid interest I'd suddenly aroused in him. I've always liked stairways, with their people who go dragging their breath up them and fall dully down them in a shapeless mass. Maybe that's why I chose the stairs to suffer on.

Thursday 10

Today I worked hard to finish my daily chores as quickly as possible: tidy up the apartment, wash my underwear, make lunch, clean my pipe ... I wanted to have more time to draw up programs and choose themes for my exercise. The study of suffering—gradual and systematic like any discipline or art—is quite arduous. My neighbor watched me for a long time. Beneath the yellowish hue of the light bulb, I must've looked transparent and diluted. The daily exercise of suffering gives one the gaze of an abandoned dog and the color of a ghost.

Once again Señor Rojas's insistent stare fell upon me and the feared question arose. Useless to explain anything. I let him continue down the stairs with his question lingering. I went on with my exercise. When I heard footsteps coming up, a shiver ran through my body. I knew them well. My hands and temples began to sweat. My heart thumped desperately and my tongue felt like a piece of paper. If I had been standing, I would have collapsed like a marionette. She smiled as she went by ... I pretended not to see her, and kept practicing.

Thursday 17

I was right at the 7th degree on the scale of suffering when I was cruelly interrupted by my ever-reliable neighbor, who went upstairs accompanied by a woman. They passed so close that their clothing brushed up against me. I was permeated with the woman's perfume, a mix of musk and benzoin—dark, viscous, damp, wild. She wore a very close-fitting red dress. I watched her as they climbed the stairs, until they disappeared behind the apartment door. They were talking and laughing. They laughed with their eyes and their hands. They were passion in movement. Wrapped up in each other, they didn't even notice me. And my pain, so pure, so intellectual, was interrupted—its clean essence contaminated by a dull itch. Dark and weighty sensations fell over me. My sorrowful meditation, the product of arduous discipline, had been frustrated and converted into a miserable fervor. Damn them! I battered their footprints with my tears.

It was a true stroke of genius to measure suffering by degrees, to assign different categories and limits. Some say that pain lasts forever and never runs out; but I believe that past the 10th degree of my scale, all that's left is the memory of pain, hurting only in recollection. At the beginning of my training I believed it was best to ascend the scale gradually. Very quickly I found this to be a poor experience. The knowledge and perfection of pain requires flexibility, a wise application of its categories and nuances, and an arbitrary rehearsal of its degrees. To move with ease from the 3rd to the 8th degree, from the 4th to the 1st, from the 2nd to the 7th, and then run through them in rigorous ascending and descending order ... I hate to interrupt this interesting explanation, but there's water beneath my feet.

Monday 21

First thing this morning the landlord showed up. I still hadn't finished mopping up the apartment. He shouted, gesticulated, said terrible things. Accustomed as I am to enduring injustices, foolishness, and mistreatment, I found his attitude to be like that of so many others. It would take a genuine artist to move me, not a mere monster in training. I didn't attach the slightest importance to him. While he was shouting, I applied myself to trimming my nails, carefully and without haste. When I finished, the man was crying. That didn't move me either. He cried the way anybody does when they need to. If he had cried as I do, when I reach my 7th-degree meditations! ...

With all humility I'll confess that I am a virtuoso of pain. Tonight while I was suffering, balled up on the staircase, my neighbors' cats came out to watch me. They were astonished that humanity could have such capacity for suffering. But I hardly noticed them there. Their eyes were like blinking torches, lighting up and extinguishing themselves. I surely must have reached the 10th degree. I lost all count, because the paroxysm of pain, like that of pleasure, envelops and clouds the senses.

Wednesday 30

I'm so somber, so thin and gaunt, that sometimes a stranger coming up the stairs becomes hysterical at the sight of me. I'm satisfied with the way I look. It is a faithful testament to my art, to its near perfection.

Sunday, August 3

I don't have the words to describe what happened today. I shudder to recall it. I still can't get over the surprise from a few hours ago. The sense of remorse I so often practice feels new again; it has made me its prey. It's as if it had been created just when I'd mastered the full scale, when I'd become a true artist. I've fallen into an unpardonable error, a betrayal of my vocation, unheard-of and disastrous. If for even a moment I had relaxed, wavered in my devotion to this demanding art, I'd say that this was the logical consequence, but I've been faithful, observant ...

I don't know if I'll ever get through this ill-fated trial. To-day I worked for three hours without stopping (which is exhausting and excessive) on the 6th degree of my scale, the most appropriate for cases like this. I've never suffered like that before: my neighbors had to pick me up unconscious at the bottom of the stairs. Here, beneath my bandages, is the clotted blood, the opened flesh. I'll have to expand my scale, or include this business of real wounds as a variant of the 5th degree. It hadn't occurred to me before—perhaps falling down the stairs was a stroke of divine inspiration. An opening of my eyes to new methods.

Tuesday 12

I haven't been able to forget. Perhaps it's a punishment for my arrogance, since I was beginning to feel confident of my abilities, to dream that I was mastering this vocation. I wrote that on Saturday, July 26. Fateful confession! Words are always treacherous and they turn against you! If only I had thought of that! I've had to practice the 6th and 9th degrees to the point of exhaustion, two hours each. Then I had to flee to my apartment in a hurry, for fear that it would happen again.

Friday 15

It happened again! Just as the last rays of the afternoon sun bathed the steps. I still feel her hand in mine, which fled from her touch. Her warm, smooth hand. She said something. I didn't hear. Her words were like soothing balm on my sores. I didn't want to know anything. It was forbidden to me. She was saying my name. I didn't listen. My efforts, my intentions, my entire art would shatter before her doe eyes, her docile animal gaze. Art is sacrifice, renunciation; vocation is vital, a mark of fire, a shadow that takes possession of the body that projects it, enslaving and consuming it … Not once did I turn my head to look at her!

Monday 18

I tore the bandages off—my blood stained the rug. I bleed inside too. I remember the warmth of her hands—those hands that may be caressing another face right now. For the first time in a long while I didn't go out to sit on the stairs; I was afraid she might arrive at any moment. I was afraid she might dispel my pain with her mere presence.

Saturday 23

In the morning Señor Rojas came. He thought something had happened to me since I wasn't in my usual corner of the stairway. He brought me some fruit and a bit of tobacco; nevertheless, I suspect he's not sincere in his concern. There's something secretive and shadowy in his demeanor. Maybe he's trying to buy my silence: I've seen the women he brings to his apartment. Maybe he wants …

Tuesday 26

In order to feel closer to the stairway, I practiced the 4th and 7th degrees next to the closed door. I heard her footsteps pause several times on the other side of it; I felt the heat of her body through it. Her perfume seeped into my lonely room. From outside she disturbed my solitude, violating my defenses. I understood between sobs that I loved her.

Friday 29

I love her, yes, and yet she's my worst enemy. The one who can put an end to what constitutes my reason for being. I've loved her ever since I felt her hand in mine. If I were a common, everyday individual like Señor Rojas or the landlord, I would sleep with her and be shipwrecked by her tenderness. But I owe myself to pain. To the pain I practice day after day until achieving its perfection. To the pain of loving her and seeing her from afar, through a keyhole. I love her, yes, because she slips smoothly along the stairway like a shadow or a dream. Because she doesn't demand my love and only occasionally peeps into my solitude.

Sunday 31

If it were only the pain of renouncing her, it would be terrible—but magnificent! That kind of suffering forms a branch of the 8th degree. I would practice it every day until I'd mastered it. But it's not just that—I'm afraid of her. Her smile and her voice are stronger than my resolve. I'd be so happy seeing her come and go through my apartment with the sun sliding over her hair ... That would be my ruin, my absolute failure! With her, my hopes and my ambition would be finished. But if she were to disappear ... Her sweet memory would gnaw away at me for the rest of my life ... Oh, ineffable torture, perfection of my art! Yes! If tomorrow I were to read in the newspapers: "Beautiful Young Woman Dies in Accidental Fall from High Staircase" ...

The Cell

WHEN MARÍA CAMINO came down to breakfast, her mother and her sister, Clara, were already sitting in the dining room—but her mother, Señora Camino, never began eating until both her daughters were at the table. María arrived silently. Leaving her bedroom, she had noticed the sound of her own footsteps: it seemed that she made a lot of noise as she walked. And she didn't want to call attention to herself or be noticed today: no one must suspect what was happening to her. She felt a deep sense of unease upon seeing her mother and sister already in the dining room, waiting for her. Her mother would ask her why she was so late, why she had kept them waiting. She entered the dining room self-consciously. When she bent down to kiss her mother on the cheek she saw her own face reflected in the big Italian mirror: it was very pale, with dark circles under the eyes. Soon her mother and sister would notice too. She felt a chill course down her spine. Señora Camino didn't ask her anything, but she was sure to at any moment, and María would need to have some excuse ready. She would tell them that her clock had stopped. She peeled an apple, aware that her mother and Clara were watching her—perhaps they were already suspicious. She lowered her gaze, conscious that she was blushing. But fortunately, just then Clara Camino started talking about a fashion show her club was organizing for charity.

"I'd love it if you came with us," she suddenly said to María.

"Of course she'll go," Señora Camino hastened to assure her, before María could say anything.

María smiled weakly at her mother and went on drinking her chocolate. She would have to talk about something too; she would have to make conversation with her mother and sister, but she was afraid that her voice would give her away and that they would realize something was going on. And she could never tell anyone. Her mother would die if she heard such news, and Clara might not believe it.

"Don't you want some marmalade?" she ventured to ask her mother, timidly passing the orange marmalade she'd made the day before.

"Thank you, dear. Ah, it's the one you made!" said Señora Camino, and she looked fondly at her daughter.

That had been yesterday, but it seemed like the distant past. She had made jams and baked cakes, knitted by her mother's side, read for hours, and listened to music. Now she could no longer do those things, or anything at all. She would have no peace or tranquility now. When they finished breakfast, María went up to her room and wept dully.

In the evening, Señora Camino and Clara almost always played cards with Clara's fiancé, Mario Olaguíbel, and his cousin José Juan. María didn't like card games—she found it all so boring and pointless. While the others played, María sat by the fireplace and silently knitted. And she only interrupted her work to serve some cream liqueur or spirit that her mother requested. That night María asked if she could play with them. They all seemed very surprised, and Señora Camino was extremely pleased: "Our little María is starting to be more sociable." She'd thought the game might manage to distract her a little. But her effort was useless. She couldn't concentrate and played clumsily. She constantly checked the clock over the fireplace, cast glances at the doors, heard footsteps. Every time she played a hand poorly, she grew flustered and blushed. Señora Camino puffed on her long ivory cigarette holder.

"Let's go, darling, come on, think about your plays," she said, every now and then, so as not to embarrass her.

José Juan smiled as if wanting to encourage her.

"Next time you'll play better, don't worry," he said when he left.

María slowly climbed the stairs to her room, and when she opened the door she was surprised by that presence ...

Señora Camino was clearly pleased to see that María was keeping busy: "That girl, who looked so worn out all the time, with no energy for anything, is now constantly active." María had succeeded in her aim: her mother and Clara believed that her health had improved and that she was happy and industrious. It was the only way to keep them from suspecting what was going on. She spent hours tidying the attic and the pantry, dusting the library, putting the closets in order. They believed she was keeping herself busy— they were never able to catch that look of distress casting a shadow over her face, or the trembling of her clumsy hands. María couldn't, even for a second, banish that image from her mind. She knew she was doomed, as long as she remained alive, to suffer this awful torture and keep it silent. The days seemed short, fleeting, as if slipping through her fingers, and the nights were endless. At the mere thought of having to face another night, she trembled and turned pale. *He* would slowly draw nearer to her bed, and she could do nothing, nothing ...

One day, María Camino realized that José Juan Olaguíbel might be a refuge for her—or perhaps her only salvation. She could marry him, travel around, go far away, forget ... He had plenty of money and could take her wherever she wanted, where *he* wouldn't find her. Fighting her natural timidity, she became friendlier and chatted with him. María's new behavior was warmly received not only by José Juan Olaguíbel but by the entire family, which made things easier. When they weren't playing cards, they spent the evening talking. María discovered that he was pleasant to chat with. She began to feel good in his company—it took her mind off her worries. Little by little she came to know tenderness and hope. They started to make plans and think about the future: in a short time an engagement ring shone on María's finger, and the wedding was set for the next January. She wished the wedding date was sooner, so she could flee the horrible torture she had to suffer night after night; but she didn't want to awaken suspicions of any kind. Her wedding would have to transpire in a perfectly normal way, as if nothing were wrong, as if she were just an ordinary girl. At night she tried to keep José Juan with her as long as possible. As the hours passed and the time for the Olaguíbels to say good night drew closer, María would begin to feel that boundless terror of being alone—maybe *he* was already waiting for her up there in her room, and she would be unable to do anything to avoid it, unable to tell José Juan to take her away that very night and save her from this torment. But right there in front of her were her mother and Clara, who knew nothing and could never know. María watched the

Olaguíbels climb into their automobile; then she closed the door and a mute desperation consumed her ...

They'd spent October and November getting ready for the wedding. José Juan had acquired an old residence that he was renovating in luxurious style. Very pleased, Señora Camino accompanied her daughter everywhere she had to go, and helped her select her purchases. María was tired. Every day, morning and afternoon, there was something to do: pick out fabrics, furniture, dishes, go to the dressmaker, to the embroiderer, discuss the house with the architect, choose rugs, curtains, colors of paint for the rooms ... She realized with great sadness and disenchantment that this lovely game of liberation had worn her out, and that she didn't want to know any more about the wedding, or José Juan, or anything. She began to feel annoyed whenever she heard him coming by the house, which he did various times throughout the day, with the pretext of consulting her about something. His voice began to grate on her nerves, as did the light kiss he gave her when he said good night—his cold, moist lips, his conversation: "the house, the curtains, the rugs, the house, the furniture, the curtains ..." She couldn't go on, she didn't care whether she escaped or suffered for the rest of her life. She only wanted a break from this tremendous sense of fatigue, from spending all day going from one place to another, speaking with a hundred people, giving her opinion, choosing things, hearing José Juan's voice ... She wanted to stay in her room, alone, without seeing anyone, not even her mother and Clara, to be alone, close her eyes, forget everything, not hear a single word, nothing, "the house, the furniture, the rugs, the white clothing, the curtains, the house, the dressmaker, the furniture, the tableware ..."

The December cold crept in, and one evening Clara made *ponche*. María, entirely distant, sat embroidering by the fireplace. Señora Camino and Clara played Uruguayan canasta with the Olaguíbels. José Juan talked about a trip he had to make to New York on family business, which was extremely annoying since it was so close to the wedding date, and especially with so many things still to arrange. When María heard this news, she felt a sudden spark of joy at the mere thought of being free of his presence for a few days. She felt the cage that had begun to close around her suddenly breaking apart. She drank several cups of *ponche de naranja*, laughed at everything, and gave him a kiss good night.

The next day María awoke feeling light and happy. During breakfast, Clara noticed that her eyes were bright and that she was smiling without realizing it.

"You have the look of a satisfied woman," she told her.

In that moment, María understood everything. And she knew why she was so happy. She had been claimed forever. Nothing else would matter now. She was like ivy attached to a gigantic tree, submissive and trusting. From that moment, the day became an enormous wait, an endless desire ...

But José Juan Olaguíbel didn't leave for New York. María saw him arrive that night, and such fury seized her that she went completely dumb. She paid no attention to anything he explained to her, tense with wrath. He didn't notice the hate in her eyes. While José Juan talked and smiled in satisfaction, she wished she could ... Without caring about what her mother and her fiancé might think, she ran upstairs to her bedroom. There she wept with rage, with vexation ... until *he* arrived and she forgot everything ...

On New Year's Eve, Señora Camino prepared a splendid dinner. Only their closest family members and the Olaguíbels came. Clara looked beautiful and happy. They had decided, she and Mario, to hold a double wedding and to make the journey around Europe together. Señora Camino couldn't help shedding tears of joy, "satisfied to have found such magnificent matches for her beloved girls." María was pale and somber. She wore a close-fitting white garment of Italian brocade, long like a tunic. She hardly spoke all night. Everyone else enjoyed the dinner, but María knew very well where her only happiness was to be found, and the party was long and draining. The hands of the clock didn't move. Time had stopped ...

Now, too, time has stopped ... *What a cold, dark room! It's so dark that day merges with night; I no longer know when the days begin or end. I want to cry with the cold—my bones are frozen and they hurt; I'm always on top of the bed, flung aside like a rag doll, hunting flies, spying out the mice that helplessly fall into my hands; the room is filled with the corpses of flies and mice; it smells of damp and of putrefying mice, but I don't care, let other people bury them, I don't have the time to; this castle is dark and cold, like all castles; I knew he had a castle ... How lovely to be a prisoner in a castle, how lovely! It's always night and he doesn't let anyone see me; my house must be very far from here; there was a huge fireplace in Papá's library and I used to arrange and dust the books; I want a fireplace to warm myself up, but I don't dare mention it to him, I'm too frightened to bring it up, he could get angry; I don't want him to be angry with me; I didn't say a single word to those men who came, he could show up and catch me; I hid in bed and covered my face with the blankets; we're always together; where are Mamá and Clara? Clara is my older sister—I don't love them, I'm scared of them, don't let them come, don't let them come! ... Maybe they're already dead and their eyes are open and shining like José Juan's that night; I wanted to close his eyes, it scared me* to have them staring at me—his eyes were open very wide, shining brightly ... "You'll be a beautiful bride, all white"—the moon was also white, very white and very cold, and since it's always night he comes whenever he wants; we're always together—if it weren't so cold I would be completely happy, but I'm very cold and my bones hurt; yesterday he beat me cruelly and I screamed and screamed ... José Juan got cold, very cold; I didn't let him fall, but rather let him slip down gently; he was bathed in moonlight and his eyes were staring; the rats' eyes are staring too; he went to sleep on the grass, beneath the moon; he was very white ... I was watching him for a long time ... I'd like to lean out of that window and be able to see the other rooms ... I can't reach it, it's very high and he could come at any moment and catch me, since he comes anytime, as often as he wants ... he could get angry and beat me ... That noise in the corner: it's another mouse, I'll catch it before he arrives, since once he comes I won't be able to do anything ...

Musique Concrète

"THAT LOOKS LIKE Marcela," Sergio thinks, stopping in his tracks. He turns to get a better look at the woman he barely glimpsed out of the corner of his eye while passing by the French Bookstore… "But wait, it is Marcela!" And he can't get over his astonishment at the fact that this gloomy, disheveled woman gazing apathetically at the store window is indeed his friend Marcela. He urgently has to get back to the office before six in the evening, but he stays and chats with her for a few minutes. Before saying goodbye, he can't help but ask her:

"You don't look well, have you been sick?"

"Not exactly," she says glumly. "Maybe it's because I haven't been sleeping well."

"Why don't we go for a coffee, whenever you like, and we'll have a good long talk and catch up. I'd love to do it today, but I have to look over a few things before my secretary leaves."

He walks away in a hurry, but Marcela's wilted face and her obvious self-neglect linger in his mind. He is troubled at his own behavior, feeling something like remorse for having forgotten about her, for seeing so little of her these past months. "It's absurd how busy I've let myself get with work and obligations: I can't even see the people I love anymore." Just last year he'd still been getting together all the time with Marcela and Luis, almost every Saturday night, to empty a bottle or two while listening to music or immersing themselves in conversations about anything and everything ...

"What's going on with Marcela?" Sergio wonders again while he shaves. He thinks that perhaps this change is due to time—they aren't twenty years old anymore, in fact they're approaching forty. He wipes away the lather and contemplates himself in the mirror. "It's not that. There must be something wrong, something must be happening to her." And it hurts him to think it might be something serious, serious enough to have caused such a disastrous change, without him knowing anything about it. In the shower he recollects their high school years, when he and Marcela spent all their time together: they went to the same parties, they loved walking aimlessly around the city or spending long hours killing time at cafés. "She was so willowy, and maybe a little pale, but it gave her an interesting look, she hardly wore any makeup and pulled her long chestnut hair back in a ponytail, she was a pretty girl," Sergio recalls. They'd been so close back then that it never occurred to him to wonder just what kind of affection it was that united them. Marcela was like a part of his very own self. Things became romantic once, but they hadn't let it go any further than a few innocent kisses. Perhaps Marcela had been waiting for him to decide, perhaps she'd grown tired of waiting and one day she became Luis's girlfriend, who knows ... "Maybe she hadn't slept yesterday, or she was a little sad and didn't feel like fixing herself up, maybe it's nothing; she's the same as always, and I'm the one who's blowing things out of proportion. How nice it would be if it were only my imagination!" And he starts reading the newspaper over breakfast until all thoughts of his friend evaporate.

He arrives at his apartment, tired after the workday, and since it's still early he calls Marcela to set a date. One, two, three rings, he wants to hear Marcela's voice, cheerful as always: "Oh, it's you, Sergio, what a pleasure!" After one more ring Marcela herself answers, but it's not the voice he knows—not the voice he's hoping to hear, needs to hear. Of course she's happy that he's calling her, he feels it, he knows it for certain, but something is definitely wrong with her. They agree to meet the next day. Discouraged, he paces in the living room. It annoys him that Velia is out of town. At least he might have shared his concerns about Marcela with her. But the poor thing is so clueless sometimes; she could have come back by now, two weeks are more than enough to get a tan and flaunt yourself on the beach ... He decides to read for a bit and looks for the book by Miller. He stretches out in an easy chair; his left leg aches a little, and he rubs it with his hand—it's annoying that after all this time it still aches when it's cold, Miguel doesn't believe him when he complains about it and never prescribes anything. "What a hassle doctors are ..." He remembers when he'd broken his leg. Marcela was the only person who regularly spent time with him during those long afternoons in the hospital, everyone else soon grew tired of visiting him; even Irene left to visit her mother in San Francisco. Marcela always showed up exhausted: "Luis is coming tonight. We bought you this book. Luis says it's great and that you'll like it ..." She would sit down with difficulty—she was expecting her second child then—and tell him all the news, the gossip about their friends; she would plump the pillows or read to him, without pause, until the afternoon had passed and the nurse arrived with the tea trolley. Luis always came to pick her up, they would chat awhile longer, and then the two would leave holding hands, with their air of timid lovers that so amused him. The day they'd married, Sergio had been as nervous as the groom himself; maybe a bit more, since Luis was always so relaxed. He'd thought that Luis would never finish getting dressed, that they would arrive late—and then they lost the rings and once they were close to the church he ran a red light and they were nearly hauled to the police station; when they finally showed up they found everyone on edge ...

A little after seven thirty that night, Sergio enters the Café del Ángel and finds Marcela sitting at a table in the back.

"Have you been waiting long?" Sergio asks, noticing that Marcela's coffee is completely cold. "I can't help it, I'm always late." He takes one of Marcela's hands and holds it between his own.

"Don't worry," she says, "I didn't remember if we'd agreed to see each other at six thirty or seven thirty, so ..."

"It's almost normal for something like that to happen to me," Sergio jokes, "but you, with that incredible memory I've always been so jealous of ..."

Marcela says her memory isn't the same anymore, that she forgets all sorts of things or gets them confused. Sergio stares at her, trying to figure out what's wrong with her; but, giving up, he asks: "What is it, Marcela, what's happened to you?"

She pulls out a cigarette and says nothing. Sergio calls the waiter and asks for two coffees.

"I don't know, everything's been so mixed up, so unexpected, like an awful dream, a nightmare. Sometimes I think I'm going to wake up and find that everything is still in one piece."

She plays with her wedding ring, turns it nervously around her finger, takes it off, puts it on, takes it off again.

Sergio suspects that it must have something to do with Luis, something painful that's hard for her to say out loud. He's uncomfortable too—the café is full of people, full of noise, it feels like the wrong place.

"I'm going to pay the check," he says. "We'll go to my house."

Marcela doesn't respond but accepts with her gaze. On the drive back, the two of them talk about things that don't particularly interest them: have you read this book, have you seen that film, the nights are colder now, it's getting dark early, the days are never long enough ... Sergio switches on the car radio; Louis Armstrong's deep, warm voice envelops them. Marcela watches the trees pass by on Avenida Tacubaya, as Armstrong sings "I'll Walk Alone."

"Do you remember," asks Sergio, "when we used to listen to this record until we scratched it?"

Marcela nods, but he knows that he can't bring her back to that time, he knows that she's stuck in another moment that she can't or doesn't want to escape from. He thinks back on those Sunday afternoons: he and Marcela and Luis in his small student's room, drinking rum and listening to Armstrong. Marcela sitting on the floor with her legs crossed and drawn up to her chin, swaying gently to the beat, Luis stretched out at her side looking up at the ceiling, and he directing an invisible orchestra, possessed, blown away by Louis ...

"It's cold," says Sergio, as he begins to arrange logs to light in the fireplace.

Marcela sits curled up in an armchair. "At least she's less tense now, but why doesn't she talk, why doesn't she tell me what's going on?" He busies himself making coffee, and in a few minutes the aroma fills the living room. He pours the coffee and begins to feel oppressed by Marcela's silence. It's the first time in all the years they've known each other that he doesn't know what to say to her. He asks if her coffee is sweet enough; she says yes. He offers her a cigarette and lights himself another. Marcela stirs her coffee, Sergio starts to blow smoke rings.

"Luis is cheating on me and everything between us is broken."

Sergio looks at her without knowing how to respond.

"It's been terrible, like suddenly finding yourself walking on a tightrope that's gone slack, and you can't situate yourself anywhere in time or space."

"Are you sure, Marcela?"

"Of course I'm sure, I confirmed it myself. At first I was confused by how detached he was acting toward me—it became more and more obvious—and by his absences. I invented all kinds of excuses. I went around and around in circles, I didn't want to see it."

"It must be something temporary, a fling," says Sergio, and goes hunting for a bottle.

Marcela shakes her head and holds out her cup to him. He fills it while thinking that women always exaggerate things. He feels cold and stokes the fire.

"I found out just a few months ago. Later I realized that it all goes back a long way, several years."

The logs burn in great orange flames whose radiance lends an even more desolate look to Marcela's gaunt face. Sergio settles himself deep in his armchair and lights a cigarette.

"Who is she?"

"A seamstress."

He tells himself that even if Marcela is exaggerating, these things do exist and they have destroyed her, they exist like these flames dancing in the fireplace. All it takes is seeing her, hearing her; she's as sad and lonely as a ruined, abandoned house. He takes a deep drink, seeing how defeated she looks—"Poor Marcela, the little girl with the ponytail!"—so much his, so much a sister to him, as if she were his arm, a part of his own body, that's how much it pains him. He tries the best he can to bolster her spirits, to give her some hope … Only death is final, everything else has a solution, things can change, this will be temporary, a painful moment—but deep inside he feels that his words are hollow, that they're good for nothing, that they're only words, wishes that won't work miracles.

He'd scheduled a business dinner, but at the last minute they tell him it's been postponed. He has the night free but doesn't feel like doing anything or seeing anyone. Marcela's situation has been plaguing him. No matter how many times he turns the problem over in his head, he can't figure out what to do to help her. Several times he's made up his mind to talk to Luis but then decided not to. Everything seems useless to him, ineffective. "It's up to them to work things out between themselves." He knows that no one changes their ways based solely on a friend's advice. He decides to go to his house and have something to eat there. When he arrives, he finds Marcela sitting on the floor by the fireplace.

"You, here … I never would have thought!" Sergio says, surprised and happy to see her.

"They told me you were going to come home late, but I had a hunch and waited."

"I'm so glad you came!" Sergio says, leaning over to kiss her cheek. "You've had me very worried."

"It's my second cognac," she says, pointing to the little glass next to her. "I've been feeling so cold."

"Yes, it is a bit cold," says Sergio, and goes to pour himself a drink. He comes back and sits by her side. "Have you talked with Luis—has he given you any explanation?"

"We've talked plenty of times," says Marcela in a discouraged voice, "but it's useless, he denies everything; he says I'm imagining it all, and each time it opens a wider gulf between us. We live in hiding from each other, like strangers, suffocated by silence."

"Maybe with time ..." Sergio begins, but Marcela doesn't let him finish.

"There's something else I didn't tell you about the other day, that's why I came today ... she's following me too."

"Who is?" asks Sergio, wrinkling his forehead.

"Her. She harasses me night after night, without letting up, for hours and hours, sometimes all night long, I know it's her, I remember her eyes, I recognize those bulging, expressionless eyes, I know she wants to finish me off and destroy me completely. I'm not sleeping anymore, I haven't dared to sleep for a while now, I'd be at her mercy, I spend my nights lying awake listening to the noises from the garden, and among them I recognize her sound, I know it when she arrives, when she comes close to my window and spies on my every move; the slightest bit of carelessness and I'd be done for—I close the windows, I check the doors, I check them again, I don't let anyone open them, she could come in through any one of them and get to me. The nights go on forever, hearing her so close, a torture that's consuming me bit by bit until the day my resistance is worn down and she destroys me ..."

"Take this, have a drink," says Sergio, holding the glass out to her. He feels that he's drawing a mental blank, that he hasn't understood correctly, and he'd like to ask and clarify things, but she doesn't give him the chance.

"When I found all of this out, I started having trouble sleeping, and I would spend all night tossing and turning in bed, hearing the sounds of the night—vague and faraway noises. I began to distinguish one sound that stood out among the rest, growing stronger and clearer, closer and closer until it reached my window, and there it would stay for hours and hours; then eventually it would leave, it would fade away into the distance, and the next night it would come back; that's how it was every night, the same sound, it wouldn't stop. Then one night I saw her—they were her eyes, I knew them, I'd followed Luis many times hoping that it was nothing but unfounded suspicions on my part, but he always went into the same building, Palenque 270, and hours would go by before he came out again; I knew that she lived there but I'd never seen her. One day they showed up together in Luis's auto; I got a good look at her, her bulging, expressionless eyes, the same eyes I'd seen beneath my window in the grass ..."

Marcela draws a hand across her forehead, trying to wipe away an image. She lights a cigarette. The clock strikes eleven; Sergio starts with surprise. He realizes it's the clock, his clock, the one that's been sitting above the fireplace for years, the one that always strikes at the hour, the same every time, but now it sounds different. He drinks a little bit of cognac, which also tastes like something else—it has a different flavor, it's as if everything, including himself, has changed. "I'm stupefied." This has all been so unusual, so confusing, that he doesn't know what to think or how to comprehend it. A thousand thoughts invade his mind like disarticulated fragments, like the disordered pieces of a motor, and he can't find the first piece, the starting point from which he could then assemble the rest. His mind is a snarled, tangled web.

"What would you do, Sergio?" Marcela asks suddenly. "Please, tell me."

To Sergio she looks like a poor creature who's been cornered and is about to bolt, and is pleading for help.

"You're very nervous, you're overwhelmed, and when you find yourself feeling that way, everything seems worse than it really is ..."

"No, Sergio, it's not my nerves, it's her there beneath my

window every night, that croaking and croaking and croaking, all night long ..."

"What are we talking about, Marcela?" asks Sergio, anguished. "I mean, whom are we talking about?"

"About her, Sergio! About the toad that's stalking me night after night, just waiting for the opportunity to come in—and tear me to pieces, take me out of Luis's life forever."

"Marcela, dear, don't you see this is all just a fantasy? A fantasy caused by exhaustion, by insomnia, by being so wrapped up in yourself, by the pain you're feeling ..."

"No, Sergio, no."

"Yes, dear, the toad doesn't exist—or rather, toads do exist, of course, but not the one you think, not her. It's just a normal toad that's gotten into the habit of coming to your window every night ..."

"You don't understand, Sergio, everything's so hard to explain, that's why I hadn't told you. I didn't, I still don't know how to say it ..."

"I understand you, Marcela."

"You don't understand me, you don't want to understand me. You think it's my nerves, or maybe that I'm crazy ..."

"Don't say that—I only think that you're extremely nervous and you're falling apart."

Marcela, who has been sitting this whole time in the same position with her legs drawn up, rests her head on her knees and starts to sob. "It's the same pose, the same pain as the night she found out about her grandmother's death," Sergio thinks, and silently he begins to stroke her hair. He can't find the words that might soothe her; he feels clumsy and maimed, as if his inner reserves have suddenly been exhausted and all that's left is a dullness, an overwhelming heaviness (he hears the doorbell), all he knows is that he's suffering along with Marcela, as much as she is and for her sake (he hears the doorbell again); he who has always protected himself from suffering and has fled instinctively from everything that might hurt him—here he is now totally destroyed, reduced to shit (once more the doorbell). "Who could it be?" he wonders with annoyance.

"Someone's ringing," says Marcela, lifting her head.

"Yes," answers Sergio.

"I don't want to see anyone; I'll go out through the kitchen."

"Wait, we don't have to open the door."

The doorbell rings again and a woman's voice calls Sergio's name.

"It has to be Velia!" says Sergio, irritated. "She's the only one capable of making such a racket."

They decide the best thing to do is let her in before she wakes the whole building up with her shouting. Sergio opens the door and Velia rushes inside. She greets Sergio with a kiss, and then Marcela, who hasn't moved at all. Like mute spectators, they watch her take her coat and gloves off while she explains that she wasn't able to announce her arrival beforehand. While passing by his house she saw a light on in the apartment and decided to drop in for a surprise visit and, since he didn't open, she started to get nervous and was worried that something had happened to him. "What could possibly have happened to me? We didn't want to see anyone," thinks Sergio, irked, and he's about to tell her so, but then his eyes meet Velia's green eyes, and his tension and bad mood subside: he simply says they didn't think it was her. Velia notices that Marcela has been crying, and she tries to find out what's wrong, but Marcela doesn't have the heart to speak.

"I felt sad," is all Marcela says; she excuses herself almost immediately and Sergio walks her down to her car.

"I'll call you soon," and he kisses her on the cheek.

He returns to the apartment, in no rush. Velia's presence annoys him; it's true he missed her and wanted her to come back, but not right at this moment when he needs to be alone with his jumbled thoughts.

"It's so good to see you again," Velia says, embracing him. Sergio gives her a light kiss and they sit close together.

"It's been days and days," says Sergio, just for the sake of saying something, and he indifferently strokes Velia's tanned arm, thinking, "You could've come back last week, but you had to show up now, when I'm a mess and I'm not in the mood for anything, not even you."

"What's going on with Marcela?"

"She told you, she was sad and started crying."

He fixes some drinks and hears Velia saying she thinks Marcela isn't looking well at all, as if there's a shadow hanging over her, as if she's completely lost interest in her own person and in everything around her.

"Yes, it's clear that she's gone through something," says Sergio, coming back with the drinks.

"And something's going on with you too, something you're not telling me ..."

Sergio doesn't answer. He sips his drink. How can he explain something that he himself doesn't understand, something that's going round and round inside him and that he can't manage to pin down or put a stop to? Velia insists on knowing what's happening and asks again and again.

"I'm worried about Marcela," Sergio begins, and he ends up telling her about the entire problem—that is, what he's been able to grasp of it: Luis is cheating on her and this has been an awful blow for poor Marcela—she's taken it terribly; she's stopped sleeping and her nerves are completely shot; she's being tormented and haunted by Luis's lover,

46

but he's sure it's only in her mind. That's all Sergio tells her—the story of a romantic triangle that's roughly the same as a million other stories of the same genre. But he knows there's something more to it, something he's not even telling himself, and he wants to be alone so he can go back over his conversation with Marcela in his head, reconstruct everything she's said to him. But Velia doesn't leave, and the rest of the night must go on as if nothing had happened. They have a few more drinks, Velia tells him about her vacation: the weather was incredible, the water deliciously warm, everyone was there in Acapulco, it's a shame Sergio didn't go, he would've had a great time; he might not believe it, but he missed out on loads of fun … They prepare some supper, eat, and make love. Later, while Velia sleeps by his side, Sergio listens to the sounds of the night and thinks about Marcela again with distress: "Right now she must be living through another of those nights that are driving her insane."

Sergio and Velia meet at a bar on Reforma where they often go. He looks disinterestedly at the people coming and going. The young women like carbon copies, their hair piled up *a la italiana*, their eyes heavily lined and their lips pale; the men with their bow ties and tailored suit jackets.

"And Marcela, have you heard anything from her?"

Sergio says he's been very busy and hasn't had a chance to get in touch.

"I think that with a little time she'll get over it," says Velia. "She'll forget about everything, even Luis—don't you think so?"

"Marcela lives in a very peculiar world, full of fantasies, that's why I'm so worried about her."

"But she's not a girl anymore, Sergio. Fantasies belong to childhood, it's absurd to be so cut off from reality at her age."

Sergio lets her speak, recognizing that it's the same thing he's been saying for days and days. He's the first to admit how preposterous the story Marcela has concocted is, but he also knows that this fantasy is completely destroying her, and this is what is driving him to despair; somehow he has to make her understand—wake her up from this absurd dream and bring her back to reality... He realizes that Velia is no longer talking and is watching him attentively.

"I got caught up thinking about Marcela," he says sheepishly, and caresses her cheek.

She smiles with indulgence.

Very early in the morning, the phone rings. Sergio jumps out of bed as if bitten by a tarantula. Marcela apologizes for having woken him up, but she needs to see him, it's very urgent. He can sense it, too, in her tone of voice, faltering and breathless.

"Come as soon as you can, right now."

He jumps into the shower to wake himself up completely. He'd been planning to sleep in, like he does every Sunday, but he doesn't regret it, once and for all he'll speak with Marcela—and for as long as it takes. While he waits he makes coffee and toast, and calls Velia to make sure she won't come looking for him. He'll go find her after he finishes talking with Marcela.

When Marcela arrives, they sit and drink coffee by the window. "She looks awful," Sergio says to himself.

"Last night," begins Marcela, "everything almost ended, that is, it could have been my last night; someone, I think it was Lupe, left the door to the garden open, and she came in through it, I'd been listening to her croaking and croaking outside the window for hours, then the noise grew more distant until I couldn't hear it anymore—I thought she'd

48

left, which surprised me ... I relaxed a bit and began to doze off, when suddenly I began to hear the sound of something thumping, every now and then. It was coming closer and closer, closer, I got up and ran to the door of my room, and there she was in the hall a few steps from my door, just one hop away from entering—staring at me with her huge eyes that seemed to be popping out of their sockets—about to leap on top of me, I know it because her legs were folded back, ready to jump, because she was inflating herself in fury before my eyes, out of her desire to destroy me ... I immediately shut the door and turned the key; at the same moment I heard her smash against the door, croaking, croaking, moaning in her pain and rage. I was saved by one instant, a single instant. I turned the key again and waited, pressed against the door listening, she moaned painfully, then I heard her leave with that dull thumping, those short heavy leaps ... I was sweating copiously, then I fainted, and when I came to, it was already daytime. I got into bed and tried to warm myself up, I was very cold and frightened, but it didn't work. I kept trembling from head to toe, then I called you ..."

With automatic movements Marcela brings the cup of coffee, which she hasn't touched, to her lips.

"It must be cold," says Sergio. "Don't drink it, I'll heat it up." And he walks to the kitchen thinking: "How to begin, what do I say to her?"

He returns with the hot coffee, pours a cup for Marcela, and another for himself. The sun shines in and bathes the living room, it's nine thirty in the morning on a Sunday in the month of October, everything is real, quotidian, as real as the woman sitting in front of him stirring her coffee, as real as he is, savoring his weekly day of rest. What is out of place, at this hour, are the words, the world that she is expressing.

"You're letting yourself get carried away by your imagination and your worked-up nerves; stop, dear, it's a very dangerous path, and sometimes it's just one step, a step that's very easy to take, and then ..."

"How can you possibly say such things to me," says Marcela with deep disappointment, "that you don't understand? It's not my imagination, it's not a dream, it's not my nerves as you call them, it's a reality so terrifying that it's driving me insane, it's being so close to death that you start to feel its chill in your bones."

"Sometimes without wanting to," says Sergio, "without realizing it, we mix up truth and fantasy and fuse them together, we allow ourselves to get caught in their web—we give ourselves up to the absurd. It's like taking a trip to a city that never existed."

"I know it's hard to explain, hard to believe, but she's real, and you don't want to realize it; I recognized her eyes on that first night when I found her there among the plants below the window, I got a good look at her that day she was with Luis, with those same bulging, cold, expressionless eyes, the face too large for someone so short, stuck to her shoulders, with no neck ..."

Sergio gets up and walks through the living room, then he leans his back against the window and says: "You have to realize how illogical this situation is, it's not possible that this crazy fantasy created by your imagination could be real; you're tired, you're worn out, you're suffering."

"And the desperation of knowing that every night could be my last, I've told you that I was saved only by a split second, an instant, closing the door before she could jump on me."

Sergio realizes that she is completely trapped in this obsession, she can't break free, it's distorting everything—whatever he says to convince her otherwise will be useless.

"And now what do I do? If tonight or tomorrow or the next night could be the last? What can I do, Sergio? Pursued, stalked relentlessly, night after night, minute after minute, without the relief of sleep, always alert, listening, following her movements like I'm a prisoner awaiting my final hour in a cell. Why this malice, this determination to finish me off? She already broke me to pieces by snatching Luis away, what else does she want? Croaking, croaking, croaking horribly all night long, without stopping, her croaking is there inside and outside my ears, her stupid, sinister croaking ..."

Sergio watches her bring her hands to her head, attempting to cover her ears. He feels a powerful grief, a kind of raw tenderness that forms a knot in his throat; he knows he's about to cry, and he turns toward the window so she won't see him. Outside he sees the sunny October morning, he sees the cars pass down the avenue with its golden trees, people carrying picnic baskets to take to the country, he sees a flower vendor, a milkman, the mailman passing on his bicycle; he sees some young women walk by, almost girls, he remembers the girl with the ponytail, he'd like to go to the country, he would have liked to go yesterday, with that girl, his friend, his sister, that broken part of him covering her ears, he'd like to ...

"I'm leaving, Sergio," says Marcela, touching his shoulder. "I want to eat with the children."

Surprised, Sergio watches her go, unable to say anything. He looks out the window again: he watches Marcela's car pull out and disappear down the avenue. He dials Velia's number and asks her to come over, but as soon as he hangs up, he regrets it. He'd rather be alone, but he doesn't want that either, the truth is he doesn't want anything; maybe he'll feel better after a drink, perhaps, but there's no peace for him now;

he's suffering over Marcela as if it's a sickness he's suddenly contracted, an unbearable malady that he can't push aside because it's fixed there, hurting him constantly.

Velia finds him downcast. They walk for a while through the park filled with children and balloons. He barely talks, he lets himself be led along. Afterward in the bar he tells Velia about his fears, the futility of his efforts and how much it hurts not to be able to do anything for Marcela. When they finish eating, Velia asks what he wants to do, where they should go.

"Wherever you want, it's all the same to me."

They drive through the city, deserted as it always is on Sunday afternoons, beneath a heavy, oppressive sky ignited by a premature dusk. They drive a long while in silence, aimless, until the cool afternoon air lashes their faces like an icy whip; Velia stops the car and puts the roof up. They continue driving in no particular direction. "I should go see the seamstress," it suddenly occurs to Sergio. But what for? What would he say to her? ... Maybe talk to her about the state Marcela is in, explain how serious the situation is, perhaps insinuate that she should leave the city for a while, that it might possibly calm Marcela down, knowing she was far away might make Marcela better ... the idea seems harebrained, a charge he would never have accepted ... Poor girl! Her only crime was falling in love with someone else's husband. In the end, this kind of relationship has always inspired his pity—and why not say it?—his sympathy too: always living in the shadows without being able to show your face, embracing in the dark, on the sly, having a second-month abortion, grief-stricken and terrified, then finally cast off with the years like a sack of useless bones. Really he pities them. He thinks she must be a nice young woman, he thinks she'll be moved to compassion when she hears about the state Marcela is in. Palenque 270 ...

He asks Velia to take him to Palenque Street, where Luis's lover lives. Velia looks at him, very surprised.

"But you, what're you going to do there?"

"I don't know, but I think speaking with her is the only thing left to do, and I'm going to try it."

Velia drops him off at the corner of the building and waits for him there.

Sergio climbs up to the third floor and rings the door of apartment 15. No one answers. He worries that since it's Sunday, she's gone out. He rings again. A young woman of indeterminate age answers the door. Sergio knows it's her, and he says he wants to speak with her. The young woman stands there looking at him, somewhere between surprised and fearful. Strange and muddled noises issue from the apartment.

"May I come in?"

She doesn't respond and tries to close the door. Sergio stops her, pushing his way into the apartment. He now locates the strange sounds he'd heard when the door opened, coming from a radio. "It must be *musique concrète* or something like that, maybe Radio Mil's Sunday program," Sergio thinks, giving a quick glance around the apartment: a long cutting table, an electric sewing machine, a black dress form, a mirror, more furniture ... The woman watches him attentively without offering him a chair. He takes a seat anyway. She sits too, placing herself in front of him, and from there she looks at him; he looks back at her in puzzlement, takes out a cigarette, and lights it. "Kind of a strange girl," thinks Sergio.

"I came to talk to you about Marcela."

"About whom?" she asks in a mellifluous and gelatinous little voice that makes Sergio choke.

"My friend Marcela, Luis's wife," says Sergio, annoyed by her stupid question.

A smile half forms on her face, somewhere between mocking and contemptuous; she says something that Sergio doesn't quite manage to hear, but something along the lines of "I don't know what you're talking about." He can't seem to hear her, because she's speaking as though she were swallowing her own words, and because the unpleasant noises, like inarticulate screams, have risen in intensity. Sergio turns toward the radio, but she doesn't lower the volume—as if the noise doesn't bother her or she doesn't even notice it. Sergio starts to talk to her about Marcela, doing his best to describe the pain his friend is feeling, her emotional collapse, her shattered nerves; he tells her everything he can—he explains, he explains again. He alone speaks: she doesn't say a word— "there's no communication, this doesn't interest her at all, nothing moves her," he thinks. She's silent, but he knows it's not an enigmatic silence, rather it's the silence of someone who has nothing to say—and the music, that is, those feverish noises, grows louder, intolerably loud, like a violent assault, surrounding them, suffocating them ... He starts talking again, explaining; he suggests that she should go away for a while, it would be the most convenient thing for everyone. She just stares and stares at him; occasionally he sees the same smile, the practiced masklike smile that stretches her lips even thinner, widening them. Sergio speaks louder and louder, to make himself heard; she looks at him as if mocking his effort; he can't stop staring back—her face is too large for someone so short, she barely has a neck, it's as if her head were stuck directly onto her shoulders ... Now he's no longer making suggestions, he's openly asking, demanding that she go far away for a while and let Marcela recuperate; she looks at him with her bulging, cold, expressionless eyes; Sergio is almost shouting so as not to be overpowered by those sounds that seem to be coming from inside her: a sad, monotonous croaking and croaking and croaking, all night long. "Marcela's right, her eyes are popping out of their sockets, her lips are a line drawn straight across her enormous head, she's inflating herself with silence, with the words she hasn't said, the words she's swallowed, she's inflated herself and she's looking at me with cold, deadly hatred, while enveloping me in her stupid, sinister croaking and croaking and croaking, with that odor of mud emanating from her, that smell of putrefied slime that's becoming unbearable; her limbs pull back, I know she's getting ready to jump on me, swollen, croaking, moving heavily, clumsily ..." Sergio's hand seizes a pair of scissors and he stabs, plunges, shreds ... The desperate croaking grows weaker, as if it were sinking into a dense, dark pool, while blood stains the floor of the room.

Sergio throws the scissors down and wipes his hands clean with his handkerchief; disheveled, he gazes at himself in the mirror and tries to fix himself up a bit. He mops off his sweat and combs his hair.

When he walks out onto the street it's already dark; he turns the corner and sees Velia's car with Velia waiting for him inside it. Before joining her, he stops in at a hole-in-the-wall shop; he buys cigarettes and dials a number on the telephone.

"Yes, it's me. You can sleep in peace now, my darling, tonight and every other night. The toad will never bother you again."

Haute Cuisine

WHEN I HEAR the rain beating against the windows, their screams return to me once more—those screams that would stick to my skin like leeches. They would rise in pitch as the pot heated and the water came to a boil. I see their eyes too, little black beads popping out of their sockets as they cooked.

They hatched during the rainy season, in the vegetable plots. Hidden among the leaves, clinging to the stalks, or amid the damp grasses; there they were plucked off to be sold—and at quite a high price. Three for five centavos generally, and, when there were lots of them, fifteen centavos a dozen.

In my house we bought two pesos' worth every week—since they were the obligatory Sunday dish—and more frequently if there were guests. With this dish my family would regale distinguished or very cherished visitors. "You won't find them more finely prepared anywhere," my mother used to say, full of pride, when they praised the recipe.

I remember the gloomy kitchen and the pot they were cooked in, which had been seasoned and given a patina by an old French chef; I remember the wooden spoon blackened with use, and our cook, a fat and pitiless woman, implacable in the face of suffering. Those heartrending screams didn't move her; she would keep on fanning the fire, blowing on the embers as if nothing were the matter. From my bedroom in the attic I could hear them shriek. It was always raining. Their screams mingled with the sound of the rain. They didn't die right away. Their agony prolonged itself endlessly. I would spend the whole time shut up in my room with the pillow over my head—but even so I could hear them. When I woke up at midnight, I could hear them still. I never knew whether they were still alive or if their screams had remained inside me, in my head, in my ears, inside and out, hammering away, tearing me apart.

Sometimes I saw hundreds of small eyes fastened to the dripping windowpanes. Hundreds of round black eyes. Shining eyes, wet with tears, pleading for mercy. But there was no mercy in that house. No one was moved by the cruelty that went on there. Their eyes and their screams followed me, and they still follow me, everywhere.

A few times I was sent to buy them, but I always returned empty-handed, swearing I hadn't found any. One day they became suspicious of me and I was never sent again. After that the cook went. She would come back with a bucket full of them; I would gaze at her with a contempt reserved for the cruelest of executioners; she would wrinkle her pug nose and huff disdainfully.

Preparing them was a very complicated affair and it took time. First she would place them in a box along with some grass and give them a rare herb that they ate—apparently with pleasure—and that served as a purgative. There they spent a full day. The next day they were bathed carefully—so as not to damage them—then dried, and placed in the pot full of cold water, fragrant herbs and spices, vinegar, and salt. When the water heated up they would begin screaming,

screaming, screaming ... They screamed sometimes like newborn children, like crushed mice, like bats, like strangled cats, like hysterical women ...

That time, my last in that house, the banquet was long and savored with pleasure.

Oscar

THE YOUNG WOMAN handed her ticket to the attendant and waited patiently for him to return with her luggage. She sat on a bench and lit a cigarette, perhaps the last she would smoke for a while, during her stay with her family. Her eyes studied the premises, trying to discern whether anything had changed in the years she'd been gone. But everything was the same. Only she had changed—and considerably. She remembered how she'd been dressed when she left for the capital: her long, loose dress, her face scrubbed and her hair in a ponytail, low shoes and cotton tights ... Now she wore a smart black sweater, a well-tailored pencil skirt that hugged her figure, black heels, and a beige trench coat; discreetly made up and with her hair stylishly arranged, she was attractive, even beautiful, and she knew it—that is, she had discovered it as she learned to dress and make herself up ...

The attendant brought her the two suitcases and said: "If you want, the mail car can take you into town, it only costs two pesos—the bus won't come for a while."

The young woman took her seat next to the fat driver and gave him the address.

"Don Carlos Román's house?" the driver asked, smiling. "I play in the municipal band with him on Sunday afternoons, and take him home afterward. If you don't mind, I'm going to stop at the post office to drop off my mailbag, I'll be no time at all."

The man went into the post office with the almost empty mailbag. From where she was sitting she could see the old town church with its slender towers, the Plaza de Armas with its kiosk and wrought-iron benches and, next to the church, her father's notary office. No doubt he was bent over a sheet of paper right now, writing with a fountain pen in his fine, uniform script.

The young woman paid the driver his two pesos, and she stood there a moment at the door before making up her mind to knock, contemplating the notary's house—her own house. After her time in the capital it seemed so small and modest, but here it was considered grand with its two floors and its cellar, rare features in the town. The paint was chipping, the windows and door were faded; it'd clearly been some time since anyone had looked after the place. Finally she knocked on the door, her heart racing as she waited.

"Monica!" Cristina cried when she saw her, hugging her affectionately. The sound of more footsteps pulled them apart, and Monica ran to throw her arms around her mother, that lean little woman with her ashen face and dull, sunken eyes. Embracing her, she noticed how extremely thin her mother was, how withered and worn-out her face, and she clasped her more tightly, feeling tenderness and sorrow.

"It's so good to see you back, dear!" said her mother, wiping away a tear.

"And Papá? And Carlos?"

"Papá is at the office, and Carlos is still at school. He's teaching the fifth grade now."

"And ... Oscar?..."

"Same as ever," her mother said laconically, sighing. In

that moment her face seemed more ashen and her eyes more sunken.

When she went into the bedroom she'd shared with Cristina for so many years, Monica felt a pang of remorse at not having brought her sister along when she left for the capital, and instead leaving her behind to languish, to waste away in this confinement. The room was the same: the two brass beds with their white knitted bedspreads, crisp and tightly stretched, as if they had just been tucked over the mattresses; the old bird's-eye maple wardrobe they had inherited from their grandmother; the marble-topped dresser with its porcelain washbasin and water jug; the bureau with its gold-plated candlestick and its candle ready to be lit, and the vase filled with jasmine blossoms that Cristina had cut to welcome her, knowing how much she loved their scent.

"Cristina, sister, you don't know how much I missed you!" Monica said with sincerity. In that moment she saw clearly that she'd missed Cristina more than anyone else. Her family, her house, the town, it was all Cristina: slim, pale, always silent, industrious, long-suffering, resigned.

"Me too, you can't imagine how much!" And Cristina's eyes grew misty. "The only thing that cheered me up was thinking you'd come back—but are you going to stay? You're not going to leave again?"

"We'll talk later, Cristina."

"You're right. I'm going to help Mamá finish cooking. Rest a little; you look tired."

Monica looked at herself in the mirror over the dresser. Cristina was right: she looked tired, and she was. Her fear of facing the rest of the family had made her extremely tense and nervous. But it was something she had to do because she very much needed the closeness and affection of her loved ones. She began to unpack her bags and hang her dresses in the old wardrobe, next to Cristina's. Hanging there side by side, those garments spoke volumes about the two young women who wore them and the circles in which they moved.

At around two in the afternoon her father and brother came home. They gave her a polite but frosty reception. Monica hadn't expected anything different. Immediately after washing their hands they sat down at the table. Her father said a brief prayer, as always, and they began to eat. How good her mother's cooking tasted to her, and how much meticulous care was put into it! They never spoke a lot during meals—it bothered her father and put him in a bad mood. Monica observed him out of the corner of her eye: in truth, he hadn't changed much, maybe he was a little thicker around the middle and a little more bald, but he was just as silent and methodical as ever, just as correct and orderly; with his napkin tucked into his shirt collar, he still slurped his soup the way he always had. At the other end of the table her mother served the meal in silence. "She hasn't just changed," Monica said to herself, "she's completely done in." Emaciated in the extreme, with her sharp, ashen face and her dull, sunken eyes, she seemed more like a sorrowful shadow than a human being. Cristina, weighed down by silence, solitude, and despair, was an aged youth, a wilted flower. And Carlos, abstracted, withdrawn, had aged as well and looked older than he was. Monica felt a great tenderness and sorrow for them all, along with pleasure at having returned. A noise like dishes falling to the floor sent a shiver up her spine. The others looked at each other without surprise.

"He must've finished eating," said their mother, rising from the table. She hurried off and disappeared through the door that led to the cellar. In a few minutes she returned carrying a tray with shards of broken plates and glasses on it. She was panting slightly and a bit of color had risen to her face.

"He's very agitated, I think it's because ..." and her eyes landed on Monica. "You should give him something, Papá."

Their father finished eating quickly, wiped his mouth with his napkin, poured a little water into a glass, and headed toward the cellar. Her brother got up from the table, grabbed a few books, and left.

The day after she arrived, Monica began to do her share of the housework, just as she had before leaving for the capital. Back to the same routine as always: at six thirty in the morning they got up; their mother fed the birds and cleaned the cages; the two sisters set the dining room table and made breakfast, and at eight everyone sat down to eat. But before that they brought Oscar his breakfast, because he'd spend the day in a terrible mood if he wasn't waited on first, and from the cellar he had an intricate knowledge of the house's noises and its schedule: he knew exactly when they woke up, when they went into the kitchen, when they went out, everything. At eight thirty Carlos headed to the school, and shortly afterward their father left to open the office. Then the three women thoroughly cleaned the house. Cristina was in charge of putting the kitchen in order and washing the dishes, their mother dusted the living and dining rooms, and Monica took care of the bedrooms and the bathroom. While their mother went out to buy groceries for the afternoon meal, the young women swept and mopped the patio and the vestibule. Then, when their mother returned with the shopping, Cristina helped with the cooking and set the table, and Monica washed the dirty clothes. In that house there was always something to do: when they finished the afternoon meal, they cleared the table and cleaned the kitchen, mended and ironed the clothes, and only later, after dinner, when everything had been picked up and put away, and their father had taken out his cello and begun to rehearse the pieces for that Sunday's concert and their brother was correcting homework, would the three women sit down to some knitting or embroidery.

From the cellar, Oscar directed their lives; so it had always been and so it would continue to be. He was the first to eat—no one was allowed to taste their food before him. He knew everything, saw everything. He shook the iron door of the cellar with fury, and shouted when something displeased him. At night he indicated, with sounds and signs of objection, when he wanted them to go to bed, and often when he wanted them to get up, too. He ate large amounts, grotesquely devouring everything with his hands, without enjoyment. At the slightest provocation he would dump plates full of food, strike the walls, and rattle the door. He rarely kept silent, always muttering an incomprehensible monologue between his teeth. When everyone had retired to their rooms, Oscar would emerge from the cellar. He would draw water from the well and carefully water the flowers in their pots—but if he was angry, he would hurl the flowerpots to the ground, shattering them; the next day all the broken pots had to be replaced, because he couldn't stand for there to be fewer of them—it was very important that there always be the same number of pots. When he finished watering the flowers he would enter the house and climb the stairs that led to the bedrooms. At around midnight you could hear the creaking of the old wooden staircase beneath Oscar's tremendous weight. Sometimes he would open the door to one of the bedrooms, just to peer in, then shut the door again and return to the cellar. But other times he entered all of the rooms, coming up to the beds and standing there for a while, motionless, watching, only his rough, heavy breathing breaking the silence of the night. Nobody moved then, they all lay rigid and paralyzed in his presence, because with

Oscar you never knew what might happen. Then, silently, he would leave the room, plod down the stairs to the cellar, and go to bed. In that house no one ever slept peacefully or normally; they slept lightly, always alert to the slightest noise. But no one ever complained: resigned to what they could not change, they accepted their cruel destiny and suffered in silence. When the moon was full, Oscar howled like a wolf the whole time and refused to eat.

You could say that the Román family was one of the most well-off in town; they had a large house of their own, a notary office, and a son who was a schoolteacher. Nevertheless, the money that father and son earned barely covered their household expenses—that is, the many expenses incurred by Oscar. Quite frequently they had to replace five flowerpots, ten, more, not to mention the dishes: they were continually buying plates, saucers, cups. Then there were the clothes and linens he ripped into shreds: shirts, pants, sheets, bedspreads, blankets; he also destroyed chairs and other furniture and, on top of all that, there were the medicines they had to constantly administer to him, which were quite expensive.

Few visitors were received in the notary's house, just a handful of relatives or very intimate friends whose voices Oscar had known well since he was little, who came on rare occasions to give their regards and to drink a cup of chocolate while chatting for a while in the waning of the afternoon. An unfamiliar person could never have entered that house; Oscar wouldn't have allowed it. The women only went out when absolutely necessary: for groceries or shopping, Sunday mass and sometimes to recite the rosary during the week, some condolence or funeral, some truly special event, because these things excited him inordinately; he didn't accept anything that would break the rhythm of his life or alter his routine. When the women went out, either their father or brother stayed at home, because Oscar feared being alone to an incredible and poignant extent and, moreover, there was always the danger that he might escape.

Monica had fallen out of the habit of going to bed early, and she would spend long hours awake, listening to Cristina's soft breathing and thinking about many, many things, until she heard Oscar's dull footsteps. Then she would lie very still and close her eyes so that he would think she was asleep. Oscar would stand by her bed for a few minutes, which to Monica seemed endless, eternal. He came to observe her every night, perhaps surprised to see her there again, or wanting to make sure it was really her. The years she'd lived in the city had made her forget this never-ending nightmare.

On that day, the sixth of August, Oscar had been unbearable since sunrise. One of the medicines he took, which calmed him down quite a bit, had run out at the pharmacy, and the doctor had substituted another that had little effect on him. He had been shouting for hours, howling, ranting, breaking everything within reach in the cellar, furiously shaking the padlocked iron door, throwing the furniture against it. He'd knocked over the breakfast tray, and the one they brought at lunch; he neither heard nor responded to anyone. "Oscar's worse than ever," their mother said when her husband and son came home to eat. "I don't know what we're going to do," she kept repeating, and she wrung her hands, overcome with anguish. "He refuses to eat, he's broken everything ..."

Without another word they sat at the table, amid the unbearable noise—the shouts and howls and roars of laughter—demolished by that soul-crushing torment. With her fingers Mamá wiped away the tears she couldn't hold back. Not even the familiar sound of Papá slurping his soup could be heard.

"He won't touch a bite, he didn't want breakfast or lunch," Mamá repeated, as if she hadn't already reported this when the notary and his son came in.

"He's smashed everything to pieces," Cristina remarked.

"I think it would be a good idea to let the doctor know what kind of state he's in," said Carlos.

Their anguish had managed to break the silence that their father had always imposed on their meals.

"—if it would be smart to increase the dosage—"

"—but ... maybe ..."

"—what should we do, oh God, what should we do?"

"—I think it's the effect of the moon—"

"—or the heat this time of year—"

"—only God knows, only God knows!—"

"—this is the worst yet—"

"—his eyes are red and bulging—"

"—he banged himself up and he's bleeding—"

"—he's been trying to open the padlock—"

"—I think the medicine's making him like this—"

"—sometimes doctors don't even know what they're prescribing—"

"—he was so calm, doing so well—"

"—yesterday he was singing, the same song all day and all night, but he was singing—"

"—yes, but last night he broke all the flowerpots—"

"—oh God, oh God!—"

"—they say there's an herbalist in Agua Prieta who's very good—"

"—sometimes they're just quacks who steal your time and money," their father cut in. "I think it'd be best to give him an injection and make him sleep, and let's hope when he wakes up the crisis will have passed. I'm going to prepare the syringe." And he rose from the table.

"I'm scared, Papá," said their mother, drawing close to her husband and clutching his arm. "Very scared."

"I've given him injections before and it wasn't a big deal—stop worrying, woman, stay calm."

"The lamp's ready," said Carlos. And the two men went down to the cellar. The women stayed there, mute and motionless, like three statues.

Inarticulate screams, sounds of struggle, of blows, of bodies falling, moans, exclamations … Suddenly it all ceased, and there was only the panting of the two men, who, bathed in sweat, emerged from the cellar, exhausted and battered, as if they had wrestled a wild beast.

The tremendous effort was too much for the notary's weary heart, which stopped abruptly the next day, as he was copying a deed at the office. He was already dead when they carried him back to his house. They kept vigil over him in the parlor all night. Though he was a well-loved and respected man in the town, only those few relatives and friends who frequented the Román house and whose voices Oscar knew were able to attend the wake. The family's sorrow was enormous; shattered by grief, they spent the entire night by the side of their deceased father, crying in silence. The next day, after the open-casket mass, he was buried; this time, at the church and the cemetery, the whole town attended. His companions from the municipal band bade him farewell by playing his favorite waltzes: "To Die for Your Love" and "Sad Gardens."

From that day forth, after Don Carlos Román died, life in that household deteriorated: the black crepe over the door and windows, the shutters half-closed, the women in mourning, silent, lost in thought, or absent, especially the mother, who seemed more like a spirit than a living woman, a phantasmal figure or the shadow of some other body; and

Carlos, downcast, mute with suffering and anguish, knowing he'd reached a dead end, cornered, hopeless; none of them had any solution for this affliction they'd endured, dragging it arduously behind them through the course of their lives. Calamity imposed itself and they were its victims, its prey. There was no salvation.

A week after the notary died, the mother fell ill; one day, that woman who'd so completely wasted away rose no more. And not even the doctor could enter the house to examine her; Oscar wouldn't have allowed it. Every day Carlos informed the doctor how his mother was doing and bought the medicines he prescribed. But it was all futile; her life slowly ebbed away, without a single complaint or lament. She spent her days plunged in a deep torpor, not moving, not talking, simply departing.

Their mother lived for only a few days, just a sigh and that was all; no death rattles, no convulsions, no tremors, no cries of pain, nothing—she just breathed a sigh and then left to follow the companion with whom she'd shared her life and her misfortune. They mourned her where they had mourned Don Carlos, and buried her next to him. After she was buried, Oscar spent the whole night in the empty bedroom, howling and gnashing his teeth.

The days of that luminous and perfumed summer marched by, long days and endless nights; the three siblings closed themselves off, didn't dare to talk or communicate, became hollow and self-absorbed, as if their thoughts and words had been misplaced, or carried away by those who had gone. Every Sunday, after attending mass, Cristina and Monica went to the cemetery to bring flowers to their dearly departed. Carlos stayed home to take care of Oscar. In the afternoons, the two sisters sat down together to knit by the parlor window, and from there they watched life go by, like prisoners through the bars of their cell. Carlos pretended to read and rocked in the rattan rocking chair, where his father had taken short naps before going to play in the concerts at the Plaza de Armas.

The full moon was immense that August night. It had been sweltering all day and the heat lingered well into the night; even the weight of a sheet on one's body was unbearable. Oscar howled like he always did on nights of the full moon, and no one could fall asleep; he howled and broke flowerpots, went up and down the stairs, bellowed, howled, shouted, kept going up and down ... Stifled by the heat, they let themselves drift little by little into sleep, a red sleep that burned like a scorching blaze, enveloping them, until they began to cough, a dry and stubborn cough that woke them up. Their eyes popping, they regarded the tongues of fire that had already reached the bedrooms, rising from the bottom floor, and the dense and asphyxiating smoke that made them cough, weep, cough, and Oscar's howls and roars of laughter — jubilant laughter like they had never heard — rising from the cellar, and the flames leaping in, almost reaching them. They had no time to lose; the staircase had been devoured by the fire, only the windows were left. Knotting sheets together, Carlos lowered down Cristina, then Monica, and finally himself. When he touched ground the house was completely engulfed in flames that burst from the windows, the door, everywhere. The sound of Oscar's laughter could still be heard as the three set off walking, hand in hand, toward the road leading out of town. Not one of them turned their head to take one last look at the burning house.

End of a Struggle

HE WAS BUYING the evening paper when he saw himself walk by with a blonde woman. He froze, perplexed. The man was himself, no doubt about it. Not a twin or a look-alike— it was he who had passed by, wearing the English cashmere suit and striped tie his wife had given him for Christmas. "Here's your change," the girl at the kiosk was saying. He took the coins and distractedly stowed them in the pocket of his suit jacket. The man and the blonde were already nearing the corner. He hastened after them: he needed to talk to them, to know who this other man was and where he lived. He needed to find out which was the real one—whether he, Durán, was the true owner of his body and the man who had walked by his living shadow, or if the other man was real and Durán only his shadow.

The couple walked arm in arm and seemed to be happy. Durán couldn't catch up with them. At this hour the streets were packed with people and it was hard to get through the crowd. Turning a corner, he didn't see them anywhere. Thinking he had lost them, he felt that anguish he knew so well, a mix of fear and anxiety. He stood looking all around him, unsure of what to do or where to go. He realized that it was he who was lost, not them. But then he caught sight of them stepping onto a streetcar. He made it aboard just in time, with his mouth dry, almost out of breath; he tried to spot them within the crush of humanity. They were toward the middle of the car, near the exit, trapped like him, unable to move. He hadn't been able to get a good look at the woman. When they'd walked by on the street, she'd seemed beautiful: a beautiful blonde, well-dressed, on his arm? ... He was anxious for them to get off the train so he could approach them. He knew he couldn't bear this situation for much longer. He saw them move toward the exit and step down. He tried to follow them, but by the time he made it off the streetcar, they'd disappeared again. For hours he scoured the nearby streets for any trace of them, but in vain. He went into different shops and bars, peered into the windows of the houses, lingered on the street corners. Nothing—he couldn't find them.

Defeated, rattled, he took the streetcar back. This unlucky encounter had increased his usual feeling of insecurity to the point that he no longer knew if he were a man or a shadow. He went into a bar—not the one where he normally drank with friends, but a different one where no one would know him. He didn't want to talk to anyone. He needed to be alone, to find himself. He had several drinks, but he couldn't forget the encounter. His wife was waiting for him to come home for dinner, as always. He didn't eat a bite. The anxious, empty feeling had reached his stomach. That night he couldn't bring himself to touch his wife as she lay down by his side, nor on the nights that followed. He couldn't deceive her. He was filled with remorse, with disgust for himself. Perhaps at this very moment he was possessing the beautiful blonde woman ...

Ever since that afternoon when he had seen himself walk by with the blonde, Durán had not been doing well. He made frequent mistakes at his job in the bank. He was constantly nervous, irritable. He spent hardly any time at home. He felt guilty, unworthy of Flora. He couldn't stop thinking about that encounter. For several days in a row he had gone to the corner where he'd seen them, and spent entire hours waiting for them to show up again. He needed to know the truth, to find out whether he was flesh and blood, or just a shadow.

One day they reappeared. He was dressed in that old brown suit that had been his longtime companion over the years—he recognized it instantly, having worn it so many times ... It brought back a flood of memories all at once. He walked close behind them. It was his own body, no doubt about it. The same veiled smile, the graying hair, his step that wore down the heel of his right shoe, the pockets always bulging with things, the newspaper tucked beneath his arm ... It was him. He followed them onto the streetcar. He caught a whiff of her perfume ... he recognized it: *Sortilège* by Le Galion. That perfume Lilia always wore and that he'd once bought for her as a gift, after going to such lengths. Lilia had reproached him for never giving her presents. He had loved her for years, back when he was a poor student dying of hunger and love for her. She scorned him because he couldn't give her the things she liked. She loved luxury, expensive places, gifts. She went out with several men, but with him almost never ... *He had arrived very timidly at the store, counting the money to see if it was enough.* "Sortilège *is a lovely fragrance," said the young lady behind the counter. "I'm sure your girlfriend will like it." Lilia wasn't at home when he went to bring her the perfume. He spent hours waiting for her. When he gave it to her, Lilia received the gift without enthusiasm, not even bothering to open it. He felt immensely disillusioned. That perfume was all that he could give her and more, and she didn't care. Lilia was beautiful and cold. She commanded. He couldn't please her* ... They got off the streetcar. Durán followed them closely. He had resolved not to approach them in the street. They walked for several blocks. Finally, they went into a gray house. They lived there, surely, at number 279. *He* lived there with Lilia. He couldn't go on like this. He had to talk to them, to know everything. To put an end to this double life. He didn't want to keep living with his wife and with Lilia at the same time. He loved Flora in a tranquil, serene way. He'd loved Lilia desperately, agonizingly, always humiliated by her. He had them both, he caressed them, he enjoyed them at the same time. And only one of them really had him; the other was living with a shadow. He rang the doorbell. He rang again ... *How patient he had been, thinking that in the long run this could win her over. He used to wait for Lilia at the door of her house, happy just to see her, to be allowed to occasionally walk her wherever she was going. Then he would go back to the boarding-house, at peace — he had seen her, he had spoken to her* ... He rang the bell again. Just then he heard Lilia scream. She screamed desperately, as if someone were beating her. And it was he himself who was beating her, cruelly and savagely. But he'd never had the courage to do it, though he'd often wanted to ... *Lilia, beautiful in a blue satin dress, looked at him coldly as she said, "I'm going to the theater with my friend, I can't see you." He was carrying the diploma he'd been awarded that day, wanting her to be the first to see it, thinking she would congratulate him for graduating with distinction. He'd told his schoolmates that Lilia would be his date to the graduation ball. "Wait a minute, Lilia, I just wanted to ask you ..." A car had pulled up in front of the house. And Lilia wasn't listening to a word he was saying. He grasped her arm, trying to keep her there just long enough to invite her to the dance. She shook off his hand and ran toward the waiting vehicle. He saw her sit very close to the man who had picked her up, saw her kiss him, heard her laughter. He felt all the blood rise to his head, and for the first time he felt the desire to take her in his arms and finish her off, to tear her to pieces. That was the first time he drank until he blacked out . . .* Again he rang the bell; no one answered. He kept hearing Lilia scream. He began to pound on the door. He couldn't let her die at his own hands. He needed to save her . . . *"All I want is for you to leave me alone, I don't ever want to see you again," Lilia had said that night, the last time he'd seen her. He had been waiting for her so that he could say goodbye. He couldn't go on living in the same place as her, suffering her slights and humiliations day after day. He had to leave, distance himself from her forever. Lilia had slammed the car door furiously as she got out. A man jumped out after her and, catching up with her, began to beat her. Durán had run to her aid. When Lilia's friend drove off in his automobile, she was crying. He had embraced her tenderly, protecting her; then she brusquely pulled away from him and said she didn't want to see him anymore. Everything inside him rebelled. He regretted saving her from that beating, he regretted showing her the tenderness he felt. If the other man had killed her, it would have been his salvation. The next day he fled from that city. He had to escape from Lilia and free himself forever from that love that belittled and humiliated him. It hadn't been easy to forget her. He saw her in every woman. He thought he saw her on streetcars, at the movies, in cafés. Sometimes he would follow a woman for a long time, until discovering she wasn't Lilia. He heard her voice, her laughter. He remembered her turns of phrase, her style of dressing, her walk, her warm, supple physique, which he'd held in his arms so few times, and the scent of her body mixed with* Sortilège. *His poverty pained him and he often despaired, thinking that if he'd only been rich Lilia would have loved him. For so many years he had relived that memory. One day Flora appeared. He'd let himself be swept along without enthusiasm. He thought the only way to be done with Lilia was to have another woman at his side. He married without passion. Flora was good, affectionate, understanding.*

She respected his reserve, his other world. Sometimes he woke up at night sensing that it was Lilia sleeping next to him; he would touch Flora's body and something inside him would tear. One day Lilia disappeared; he had forgotten her. He grew used to Flora and began to love her. Years went by... He could barely hear Lilia's screams, they were very weak, muted, as if... He forced the door open and went inside. The house was completely dark.

The fight was long and muffled, terrible. Several times, falling, he touched Lilia's inert body. She'd died before he could get there. He felt her blood, warm still, sticky. Her hair got tangled in his hands. He continued that dark struggle. He had to make it to the end, keep going until only Durán remained, or the other one ...

It was close to midnight when Durán emerged from the gray house. He staggered out, wounded. He looked around with suspicion, like a man afraid of being found and arrested.

Tina Reyes

TINA REYES SAID goodbye to the other girls from work, whom she'd walked with for several blocks, and boarded the bus that would drop her off near Rosa's house. She was lucky enough to find a seat at this hour, and she settled in next to the window. She was as tired as always when the weekend arrived: "Thank goodness tomorrow's Saturday." Only a half day of work, but then came Sunday, and she couldn't stand those Sundays: mass at 11:30, chocolate and vanilla ice cream, a double feature at the second-run cinema, which was always full of people, of bad smells and smoke; a sandwich and a Coca-Cola afterward, and Sunday would end exactly like hundreds of Sundays before it and others to come; then Monday and Tuesday and the whole workweek with no time for anything, not even to paint her nails. This is what she thought while she gazed at the walls of the bus with their weathered, peeling lacquer. "I hope Rosa's all right"—last week she'd looked very tired, it was only natural with so much work, no one but her to do all the chores and take care of the children and Santiago. Good thing Santiago was so kind to her, he gave her everything he had; the only problem was that he had no income besides his job and they were always worried about money, but he loved Rosa so much; if he didn't supply her with everything she could want, it wasn't by choice, he was truly a good man, so serious and hardworking, he never hung around with his friends or stayed out all night drinking, always straight home from work. Rosa was lucky: a husband like Santiago, her children, a small house. If you thought about it, Rosa had a lot—but she, on the other hand ... Tina sighed and shook her head, trying to divert the course of her thoughts. She didn't want to think about herself or her own life; it got her down—she always ended up depressed. Living alone, without anyone to miss her, was too painful; with nothing more than a room on the third floor of a dark and dirty building, a room so cramped that her things barely fit inside: the brass bed that she had once thought was gold, dulled by the years, the table where she ate and ironed, the sewing machine her mother had left her, and that old wardrobe she hadn't dared sell because it would have been like selling all of her memories. She'd kept her parents' clothes, her own, some savings, family portraits, so many things ... She would grow old there in that sad room, a room as sad as she was, as the despair that grew inside her day by day; everything would be different if her parents were still alive, but they'd been so old already, and so sick ... It would have been harder to watch them suffer for years and years, maybe it had been her destiny to be left alone in the world; she couldn't even keep a cat or a dog in that tiny room, and the poor canary Rosa had given her had died right away, doubtless for lack of fresh air and sunshine ... What would it be like to have an apartment, what would it be like to have a husband, children, a man to embrace her and say "Tina" in an affectionate voice?—even if she had to work as hard as Rosa did, to know that at the end of the day he'd come home. To eat dinner together while chatting about all the events of the day or about the children, to watch television afterward or, even if there wasn't one, at least listen to the radio for a bit, then to sleep with her head on his shoulder—she wouldn't feel so cold at night anymore, she'd sleep peacefully hearing him breathe. To watch the children grow up, to hear them say "Mamá" ... The tears were about to spill from her eyes, but, realizing she was in a bus full of people, she managed to pull herself together, and only a single tear rolled down her cheek. Hastily she pulled a little mirror and a handkerchief from her purse. She dried her eyes and looked out the window, very embarrassed, fearing someone might have noticed. The bus stopped at the corner in front of the Bluebeard, which in daylight appeared even more sordid, painted a garish orange and blue. The neon sign she saw every night was unlit. No question about it, this was a terrible neighborhood, as Rosa always told her, but it was close to her work and the rent was only a hundred pesos, which was all she could afford. She stretched her skirt to cover her knees, which were showing, and went back to thinking about those nights when sleep escaped her, when she spent the hours watching the luminous sign of the Bluebeard blink on and off, hearing that frenetic, insane music all night until dawn. She would see countless couples come out singing or splitting their sides with laughter; sometimes they would get into fistfights there in the middle of the street, shouting the crudest insults at each other, then they would patch things up and disappear, arms around each other, down the dark streets; other times a patrol car would come and take them away. She'd always despised those easy, perverse women; their laughter echoed in her ears, she had to cover her head with the pillow, sobbing in indignant protest until she fell asleep ... Her stop had arrived and she stepped off the bus; she was happy to find that there was still a bit of daylight left and that she didn't feel cold. It was pleasant to walk.

"Pardon me, señorita, may I walk with you?"

Tina opened her eyes wide, almost paralyzed by surprise.

"I find you quite charming—you struck me the moment you got on the bus. You have very expressive eyes."

"Excuse me, señor," Tina finally managed to say, "but I don't make a habit of talking to strangers."

"If you'll allow me to introduce myself, I won't be a stranger anymore," said the man. "Why don't you give me the opportunity? I think we'll be friends, don't you?"

Tina picked up her pace as much as she could, wanting to arrive as soon as possible at her friend's house, to spare herself from this impertinent man. She crossed a street at a red light and had to run to avoid being hit by a car. When she reached the sidewalk she breathed in satisfaction, thinking she'd managed to give him the slip.

"If we had a mutual friend, he would introduce us ..." There he was again by her side. "But I very much fear we don't have one. Won't you give me a chance?"

Tina didn't answer. She decided it would be best not to say another word to him, so that he would tire of the chase and leave her in peace.

"Really, I find you very charming," he said, undeterred by Tina's silence. "You made quite an impression on me."

Rosa's house had never seemed so far away. And what if Rosa weren't there and she found the door locked? She was always waiting for her on Fridays at this hour ...

"But it's so simple to be friends," the man insisted.

What if Rosa had gone to the doctor and wasn't back yet? Last week Rosa had said she wasn't feeling well ...

"You won't tell me your name?" the man asked.

Finally she made it to Rosa's house, and she gave a sigh of

relief when the door had closed behind her. She remained standing next to it for a few minutes until she heard his footsteps finally move away. Rosa was ironing when Tina appeared, flustered, her cheeks flushed, panting after the dash she'd made. After drinking a glass of water, Tina told her friend about the incident, in all its details. Rosa laughed in amusement and wanted to know what the fellow looked like.

"I didn't even see his face," Tina confessed.

For a while Rosa went on joking with Tina about what had happened. Suddenly she stopped and appraised her friend knowingly.

"You are looking good today, no doubt about it," she said, dying of laughter. "Really, that blue sweater is lovely on you."

Tina protested that it wasn't what Rosa thought, but, as if without meaning to, she inched toward a mirrored wardrobe and contemplated her reflection, first with a certain shyness, fearing that Rosa would notice she was looking at herself, and then carefully, with all her attention. Her hands slid over her breasts and rested on her narrow waist. She wasn't bad at all—to be honest with herself, she had to admit that she looked quite good, but how sad, what awful luck that this body, so well formed, would wither away in the shadow of solitude, without knowing a single caress, a single moment of pleasure. She couldn't help lamenting it.

"All right, stop looking at yourself so much," Rosa said.

Tina blushed and sat down in a rocking chair. She had the air of a little girl caught misbehaving. She began to rock in the chair and grin. How good she felt whenever she saw Rosa! When they chatted, the hours flew by and she forgot her sorrows. She would love so much to see her every day, like back when they were neighbors and Rosa hadn't married yet and she was living with her parents ...

They were almost definitely going to give Santiago a raise,

Rosa was saying, and with that, he wouldn't have to work overtime at night anymore. They were very happy. Apart from the fact that it meant a little more money, which would solve some things for them, they would be able to see each other more.

"There are days when we hardly see each other at all," Rosa complained.

"You don't even know how happy I am to hear this," said Tina, thinking that it was about time their finances improved, after so many years of scraping by.

Another piece of good news was that a clerk at the factory where Santiago worked was going to get married and her position would be open.

"Santiago thinks he could get it for you. Wouldn't that be fabulous?" Rosa asked.

The news thrilled Tina, because she had always coveted that job. But she also couldn't help feeling bad thinking that if she got the position as clerk, it was because the other woman was leaving it to get married. The whole world had the chance to get married, thousands of girls got married every day, except her. But she had no more time to go on thinking about her bad luck because Rosa began chatting about other things. As they were cooking dinner, Tina caught herself making plans: she was surely going to earn more money, and then she could rent a little apartment near Rosa and Santiago. How marvelous it would be to leave that horrible room forever and never again lay eyes on the Bluebeard, that sordid dive that she despised with all her soul; a different job where she wouldn't have to meet an obligatory quota, unlike the sweater factory where she had to make a hundred sleeves or collars without a chance to catch her breath ...

While they ate dinner, Rosa commented that the cold was

coming and the kids didn't have anything decent to wear. She asked Tina if she could get some sweaters from the factory at a markdown. Tina assured her she could, saying that they gave the employees a good discount. They then started to take the children's measurements and choose the most suitable colors. The kids were excited to know they would have new sweaters, and they picked colors Rosa didn't agree with. She always bought them clothing with the idea that it would last them a long time and not make them look like such bumpkins.

They had a hard time putting the children to bed, and once they'd managed it, they cleared the table and sat down to chat awhile longer. Rosa listened to a radio drama twice a week, a lovely and very interesting story; the only thing that bothered her was that sometimes she missed an installment, but since they always gave a short summary of the previous episodes at the start of the program, you could still follow the story, which was truly moving and often made you cry—even she, who almost never cried, found herself shedding tears when she listened to *Anita de Montemar*. Tina had also listened to an episode one day, when the workshop supervisor had to go out and left the radio there. He always put on baseball games or things she didn't understand, but what could she do about it?

Since it was already past nine and Santiago wasn't there to walk her to the bus, Tina decided to leave before it got much later. When she reached the corner, she had her second surprise of the day: there was the man who had followed her that afternoon. She hadn't seen his face but she remembered his height and the color of his suit. She thought about turning back to Rosa's house, but since she saw her bus pull up at that very moment, she boarded it without further hesitation. She didn't think he'd managed to get on, and she began to calm down. The bus swerved sharply and Tina nearly fell. Someone steadied her just in time. When she turned to say thank you, she saw with fright that it was the same man, and swallowed her words. He only smiled. Then she saw his face: "He's quite young and not bad-looking at all." In fact, she found him attractive, and she almost wished that, instead of a stranger, he were a friend of Santiago and Rosa's—she might have liked getting to know him under different circumstances ... "Here, Tina, this is X, he's my best friend ... X says he's very interested in you, and he's such a fine young man ... X says that once they give him a raise he'll ask you to marry him, I swear you won the lottery, he's a real catch ..." Someone asked about a stop and the fare collector answered that it was the next one. Tina realized, then, that she had taken the wrong bus. In her haste to board she hadn't noticed. The blood pounded in her temples and her legs went weak. Very shaken by what was happening to her, she stepped off onto the street.

"I was waiting for you," he said. "I had a hunch you would come back out."

Tina looked around, trying to orient herself and see where she could catch a bus that would take her back to her house.

"See, it's destiny," he said, pleased.

Those words were like a lightning bolt suddenly striking her. She felt that she had gone down a dead end, and her mind began to whirl like a spinning top. All of a sudden she remembered all the stories she had read in the newspapers: this was how they all began, it was always identical, the same thing had happened to that poor girl named Celia, she'd read about it not long ago, she remembered it very well ... She paused at the corner, not knowing what to do or where to go. She didn't see a bus stop anywhere. Across the street there was a bustling ice cream shop; she thought to ask there. Then the man said:

"May I invite you to a soda?"

She knew it was too late to try to escape; no one ever managed to outrun their destiny. She could try a thousand things and all would be useless. Sometimes destiny suddenly presented itself, just like death, arriving one day when it's too late to do anything about it. All that was left was for her to resign herself to her sad end. Convinced of her fate, she meekly let herself be led along.

They sat at the only free table and he ordered two Coca-Colas. There were lots of people and lots of noise, voices, peals of laughter, the jukebox blaring. Tina was completely dazed and very frightened.

"I still don't know your name," he said. "I'm Juan Arroyo."

"Cristina Reyes," said Tina, and instantly reproached herself for not having given another name — but then, what did it matter in the end?

"Cristina — Tina — that's a very pretty name, I like it," said the young man, smiling.

When he smiled his eyes lit up. His eyes were black, somewhat almond-shaped. "He really does have a handsome gaze," Tina couldn't help thinking. The waitress arrived with the sodas. While he poured them, she closely observed the bottles and the liquid. She was well aware, thanks to the newspapers, that her drink could be drugged — and since the sodas had been served uncapped, it would be very easy ...

"Tell me about yourself, Tina. What do you do?" the young man asked, showing an interest she knew was completely false.

Tina began to tell him, with great difficulty, that she worked in a sweater factory. She recited the words reluctantly; fear had parched her throat. She took a sip of Coca-Cola, just a swallow, enough to wet her mouth and also try to discern if it had a funny taste, but she didn't notice anything strange about the soda and this calmed her down a little. Although maybe they put something flavorless in it. They had slipped something in Celia's drink, and the poor girl didn't realize a thing until the next day when she woke up ...

The young man insisted on knowing more details about her: her family, who she lived with, what she liked to do, where she liked to go ... Tina began to exhume her dead and invent brothers and sisters. She couldn't tell him she lived alone and had nobody to protect or rescue her. If he found out, he was capable of coming into her room and right then and there ... They had suffocated one poor girl with her own pillows, in her own house, after ... "How horrible!" And icy water poured down her spine, making her shiver.

He told her that he worked at a printing press; this wasn't, of course, what he wanted, but since jobs were scarce and hard to find, he had to be satisfied with it. It had been a year since he'd come here from Ciudad Juárez, where the rest of his family lived. He had risked leaving home, thinking that there were more opportunities in the capital. He was living in the house of some distant relatives, where he went only to sleep, and he still missed his home and his family enormously ... Tina listened, knowing ahead of time that everything he said or might possibly say was false. A lesson learned by memory and practiced many times, God knew how many. All guys like him operated the same way. It seemed as though butter wouldn't melt in their mouths, and they lied up until the final moment, when they unmasked themselves with the utmost cynicism. She didn't deserve such a cruel end: her loneliness and poverty were hard enough on her. She began to feel miserable and was terribly close to breaking down and crying, and she desperately wondered what she had done, why and in what way she was going to be punished.

There were three couples at the next table. Against her will, Tina saw a woman with dyed blonde hair throw her arms around the neck of the man next to her, kissing him in front of everyone with total shamelessness. Tina immediately looked away, sensing herself blush all the way to the roots of her hair. They were just like the girls she saw come out of the Bluebeard, she couldn't understand them or excuse them—she was so different, she believed in love, in holding hands, in moonlit nights, in tender words and gazes; for a long time she'd imagined what her white dress would be like, how the church would be decorated on her wedding day and the music they would play ... She suddenly felt a terrible fear of the hours to come: Where would he take her? How would he begin? Her mind, full of anguish, was trapped in a blind alley.

"Do you want another soda, Tina?" he asked.

"No, thank you," she said.

"Really, feel free," he insisted.

Again, she refused, but then she thought it was a good idea to spend as much time as possible in the ice cream shop, because nothing could happen to her there. They drank another soda, and he went on chatting and asking questions, coaxing words from her. He conversed with a smooth and well-modulated voice, in caressing tones. "He must have a lot of practice ..." And a kind of burning tingle swept through her whole body each time she thought: How would it begin? Was he one of those men who beat girls brutally? Or perhaps with no further explanation he would pounce on her and rip her clothes off; then again, there were some who killed their prey first and afterward ... She felt very hot; she took out her handkerchief and fanned herself with it, then wiped her forehead.

He asked if she was feeling ill; Tina could barely answer no, she wasn't, but that it was very hot in there. Then the young man paid the bill and they left the ice cream shop.

"We'll have to take a cab," he said. "There aren't any more buses at this hour."

This was the usual method, what she'd read about in the newspapers—they were always in league with a taxi driver, maybe he planned to take her outside the city, bringing her to one of those sinister places ... That's what had happened to poor Celia ...

He suggested they go to a nearby corner, because taxis always passed there, at all hours. And Tina went on telling herself that of course the accomplice taxi would be there. But she let herself be carried along, convinced that this was her destiny, and that it had to be fulfilled whether she resisted or not. And sure enough, as soon as they arrived, a taxi pulled up.

When the young man asked for her address, she gave it to him without hesitation, certain that he would take her to another very different location. She settled into the back seat, shrinking against the door, and watched him out of the corner of her eye: the poor man thought he was deceiving her, as if she didn't understand what was going on. Many times she almost had the desire to laugh, but when she remembered that the end was near, she felt as though the tightrope she'd been balancing on had snapped and she was falling into the void, plunging all at once into the darkness.

"What a beautiful night!" the young man remarked, drawing closer to Tina. "I think it's the company that makes it seem that way. It's not cold at all. Did you see how big the moon is?" And he took Tina's hand between his own.

Tina's hand was cold and damp; the young man's were

warm and dry. Tina gazed outside, upward, wondering if she would ever see another night, another moon like this one, if she would come out alive, although in the end it was almost the same: if he didn't kill her, she wouldn't be able to live with what had happened. She would die of shame without ever being able to show her face—surely she would appear in the newspapers, like so many other girls who suffered the same fate. How could she look Rosa and Santiago in the eye then, how could she kiss their children ...?

"I haven't felt this happy in a long time. You look like a girl I knew in Ciudad Juárez—we were boyfriend and girl-friend, I loved her very much and I still think about her all the time. I had bad luck, they wouldn't let her marry me and we ended things. Later she married another man who took her away with him, and I haven't seen her since."

She told herself that it was only natural the parents had been opposed, surely she was a good girl and he had ...

"I love your eyes. They're so big and so pretty, like hers," said the young man, squeezing her hand.

A strange and unfamiliar feeling was invading her; she noticed all of a sudden that the young man was pressing her hand tightly between his, and she pulled it away in great shame—how had she been so careless? She tried to console herself by thinking that she wasn't to blame for everything that was happening to her; at no point had she encouraged him, she had behaved well, as always—it was fate, that's all, she was the victim of an implacable destiny, but—how would it begin? She saw herself stripped of her clothes, in a sordid room, at his mercy, and he coming closer, closer ... A hot wave of shame engulfed her and at the same time the chill of her nakedness made her shiver and shrink further into the corner of the back seat like an animal crouched in hiding.

He went on talking about how much it had struck him to see those same eyes again. At first, when she had boarded the bus, he'd mistaken her for his old girlfriend. But it was better this way, he was very happy to have met Tina, to have found her, when he felt so lonely and so bored, when he had no one to go out with, no one to chat with, and he said other things that Tina, her head spinning with her unleashed thoughts, barely heard. The moment was near and she was seized with terror. She didn't even have the possibility of calling for help and escaping. It all made her feel ashamed: What would they think of her? Maybe that she'd been asking for it, they'd probably think she was "one of those girls," and they would treat her like one ... How terrible the police stations must be, the police themselves, the endless and degrading questions — what would he say? The confrontations, the two of them face-to-face and full of hate, she the target of everyone's gaze, the photographers harassing her, the medical examination, lying completely naked on a cold table, fastened by the wrists and ankles, and all of them above her like vultures, hands, eyes, on her, inside her, everywhere, and her naked in front of a hundred eyes that devoured her — never, never, she'd rather suffer whatever happened alone, in silence, without anyone else knowing ...

The car stopped. The young man paid and they got out.

The moment had arrived and she was swept up in an enormous whirlwind of thoughts and images that thronged and spliced and succeeded one another with the speed of a cinematographic film suddenly and vertiginously unwound.

"Is this where you live, Tina?" he asked.

Tina lifted her eyes, which had been glued to the ground, and saw her building: but it wasn't, because it couldn't be, because he had taken her somewhere else, and it was her eyes that were deceiving her, that made her see what wasn't real, her room on the third floor of a miserable building, where she would have liked to arrive just like any other night, what she wished were so, but it wasn't ...

"Would you let me pick you up at work tomorrow?" the young man was saying.

But Tina would hear him no more.

She had crossed the threshold of her destiny had passed through the door of a sordid hotel room and went running down the street in a frantic desperate race crashing into people running into them all like bodies alone in the dark that meet intertwine join together separate join together again panting voracious insatiable possessing and possessed rising and falling riding in a blind race to the end with a collapse a sudden fall into nothingness outside of time and space.

The Breakfast

WHEN CARMEN CAME down to breakfast at the usual hour of seven thirty, she hadn't dressed yet, and was wrapped in a navy-blue bathrobe with her hair in disarray. This wasn't all that caught the attention of her parents and her brother, however—it was the dark circles around her eyes and her haggard face, like that of someone who's had a bad night or is very ill. She said good morning in an automatic way and sat at the table, nearly collapsing into her chair.

"What happened to you?" her father asked, studying her carefully.

"What's the matter, dear, are you sick?" her mother asked in turn, putting an arm around her shoulders.

"She looks like she didn't get any sleep," her brother said.

She sat there without responding, as if she hadn't heard them. Her parents shared a glance out of the corner of their eyes, very puzzled by Carmen's demeanor and appearance. Without daring to pose more questions, they began eating their breakfast, hoping that at some point she'd come back to herself. "She probably got a little too drunk last night— poor girl, I bet she just has a terrible hangover," thought her brother. "Those constant diets to maintain her figure must be affecting her," her mother said to herself as she went to the kitchen for the coffee and scrambled eggs.

"Today I really will go to the barber, before lunch," said the father.

"You've been trying to go for days now," his wife remarked.

"But it's such a pain even to think about it."

"That's why I never go," the boy assured them.

"And now you have an impressive mane like an existentialist. I wouldn't dare leave the house like that," said his father.

"You should see what a hit it is!" said the boy.

"What you should both do is go to the barber together," suggested the mother, while serving their coffee and eggs.

Carmen placed her elbows on the table and rested her face between her hands.

"I had an awful dream," she said in a small voice.

"A dream?" asked her mother.

"A dream's no reason to act like that, sweetie," said her father. "Come on, eat your breakfast."

But she didn't seem to have the slightest intention of doing so, and remained immobile and pensive.

"She woke up in a tragic mood, what can you do?" her brother explained with a grin. "These undiscovered actresses! But come on, don't get upset, they can give you a part in the school theater ..."

"Leave her alone," said their mother, sounding annoyed. "You're just going to make her feel worse."

The boy didn't press his jokes any further, and started talking about the protest rally the students had held the night before, which a group of riot police had broken up with tear gas.

"That's exactly why I get so worried about you," said their mother. "I'd give anything for you to stop going to those dangerous rallies. You never know how they're going to end, who's going to end up hurt, or who'll get thrown in jail."

"If it happens to you, there's nothing you can do about it," said the boy. "But you have to understand that a person can't just sit calmly at home while other people are giving everything they've got in the struggle."

"I don't agree with the tactics the government is using," said the father, spreading butter on a slice of toast and pouring himself another cup of coffee. "However, I don't sympathize with the student rallies, because I think students should apply themselves simply to studying."

"It's hard for such a 'conservative' person like you to understand this kind of movement," said the boy ironically.

"I am, and always have been, a supporter of liberty and justice," his father replied, "but what I don't agree with ..."

"I dreamed that they killed Luciano."

"What I don't agree with ..." the father repeated. "Wait, that they killed who?" he asked suddenly.

"Luciano."

"But look, dear, don't get so worked up over such a ridiculous dream, it's as if I dreamed that I embezzled money at the bank and then got sick because of it," said the father, cleaning his mustache with his napkin. "I've also dreamed many times about winning the lottery, but as you can see ..."

"We all dream unpleasant things sometimes, and other times lovely things," said the mother, "but none of them come true. If you want to interpret your dreams the way other people do, death or coffins mean long life or a prediction of marriage, and in two months ..."

"And what about the time," Carmen's brother said to her, "that I dreamed I went on vacation to the mountains with Claudia Cardinale! We were at the cabin and we were just

94

getting to the good part when you woke me up—do you remember how furious I was?"

"I don't really remember how it started ... But then we were in Luciano's apartment. There were red carnations in a vase. I took one, the prettiest one, and I went to the mirror," Carmen began recounting, slowly and without inflection. "I started playing with the carnation. Its smell was too strong, but I kept on inhaling it. There was music and I wanted to dance. I suddenly felt as happy as when I was a little girl and I would dance with Papá. I started dancing with the carnation in my hand, as if I were a lady from last century. I don't remember how I was dressed ... The music was lovely and I abandoned myself to it. I had never danced like that before. I took my shoes off and threw them out the window. The music went on and on, I was starting to feel exhausted and wanted to stop and rest. I couldn't stop moving. The carnation forced me to keep dancing ..."

"That doesn't sound like an unpleasant dream to me," her mother commented.

"Forget your dream already and eat some breakfast," her father pleaded.

"You're not going to have time to get dressed and go to the office," her mother said.

Carmen didn't show the slightest sign of paying any attention to what they were saying; her father shrugged in discouragement.

"Saturday's the dinner for Don Julián, finally. I'll have to send my Oxford suit to the cleaners, I think it needs a good ironing," he said to his wife.

"I'll send it today to make sure it's ready for Saturday, sometimes they're so unreliable."

"Where's the dinner going to be?" asked the son.

"We haven't decided yet, but most likely it'll be on the terrace of the Hotel Alameda."

"How elegant!" the boy remarked. "You'll love it," he assured his mother, "it has a magnificent view."

"I have no idea what I'm going to wear," she complained.

"Your black dress looks great on you," her husband said to her.

"But I always wear that same dress, they're going to think it's the only one I have."

"Wear a different one if you like, but that dress really does look good on you."

"Luciano was happy watching me dance. He took an ivory pipe out of a leather box. Suddenly the music ended, and I couldn't stop dancing. I tried again and again. I desperately wanted to get rid of the carnation that was forcing me to keep dancing. My hand wouldn't open. Then the music started again. Out of the walls, the roof, the floor, there came flutes, trumpets, clarinets, saxophones. It was a dizzying rhythm. A long rough shout, or a jubilant laugh. I felt dragged along by the beat, getting faster and wilder. I couldn't stop dancing. The carnation had possessed me. No matter how hard I tried, I couldn't stop dancing—the carnation had possessed me ..."

They waited a few moments for Carmen to continue, then they traded glances, communicating their puzzlement, and kept on eating breakfast.

"Pass me some more eggs," the boy asked his mother, and he looked out of the corner of his eye at Carmen, who was sitting lost in her own thoughts. "Anyone would say she's stoned," he thought to himself.

The woman served the eggs to her son and picked up a glass of juice that was sitting in front of Carmen.

"Drink this tomato juice, *hija*, you'll feel better," she said.

When she saw the glass her mother held out to her, Carmen's face distorted completely.

"No, my God, no, no! That's how his blood was—red, red, thick, sticky! No, no, how cruel, how cruel!" she said, violently spitting out the words. Then she hid her face in her hands and began to sob.

Her mother, distraught, stroked her head.

"You're sick, dear."

"That's right!" said her father, exasperated. "She works so much, she stays up every night, if it's not the theater it's the movies, dinners, parties, and look, here's what happens! They want to use it all up at once. You teach them moderation and it's 'You don't know anything about it, when you were young everything was different'—well, it's true, there are lots of things you don't know about, but at least you don't end up ..."

"What are you insinuating?" his wife said, raising her voice.

"Please," their son interrupted, "this is becoming unbearable."

"Luciano was lying on the green divan, smoking and laughing. The smoke veiled his face. All I heard was his laughter. He blew little rings of smoke. They went up, up, and then they burst, they broke into a thousand pieces. They were tiny beings made of glass: little horses, doves, deer, rabbits, owls, cats ... The room filled with little glass animals. They settled all around, like a silent audience. Others hung in the air, as if they were on invisible cords. Luciano laughed and laughed when he saw the thousands of little animals he was puffing out with each mouthful of smoke. I kept dancing, unable to stop. I barely had space to move, the little animals were invading the room. The carnation was forcing me to dance, and more and more animals came out, more and more: there were even little glass animals on my head, nesting in my hair, which had become the branches of an enormous tree. Luciano roared with laughter, a laughter I'd never heard before. The instruments started to laugh too, the flutes and the trumpets, the clarinets, the saxophones, they all laughed when they saw I didn't have room to dance, and more and more animals came out, more, more ... Finally I could hardly move. I was just barely swaying back and forth. Then I couldn't even do that. They had me completely surrounded. I looked miserably at the carnation that was forcing me to dance. There was no carnation anymore, there was no carnation—it was Luciano's heart, red, hot, still beating in my hands!"

Her parents and brother looked at each other in confusion, not understanding anything now. Carmen's perturbation had broken the rhythm of their lives like an intruder, throwing everything into disarray. They sat in silence, blank, fearful of entertaining an idea they didn't want to consider.

"The best thing for her would be to lie down for a bit and take something to calm her nerves, otherwise we'll all end up crazy," said her brother finally.

"Yes, that's what I was thinking," said her father. "Give her one of those pills you take," he ordered the mother.

"Come on, dear, go upstairs and lie down for a bit," said her mother, overwhelmed, trying to help her daughter to her feet, though she herself lacked the strength to do anything. "Take these grapes."

Carmen lifted her head; her face was a devastated field. In a barely audible murmur she said: "That's just how Luciano's eyes were. Static and green like frosted glass. The moon was coming in through the window. The cold light shone on his face. His green eyes were wide open, wide open. They were all gone now, the instruments and the little glass animals. They had all vanished. The music had stopped. Just silence and emptiness. Luciano's eyes stared at me, stared, as if they wanted to pierce through me. And I was there in the middle of the room with his heart beating in my hands, beating still … beating …"

"Take her upstairs to bed," said the father to his wife. "I'm going to call the office and tell them she's not feeling well—I think I'll call the doctor too." And he searched for approval with his gaze.

Mother and son nodded in agreement, while their eyes thanked the old man for doing what they all wished.

"Come on, dear, let's go upstairs," said Carmen's mother.

But Carmen didn't move, nor did she seem to hear.

"Leave her, I'll bring her upstairs," said her brother. "Make her some hot tea, it'll do her good."

The mother walked to the kitchen with heavy steps, as if the weight of many years had suddenly fallen upon her. Carmen's brother tried to move her, but she didn't respond at all, and, not wanting to be too forceful with her, he decided to wait. He lit a cigarette and sat down next to her. Their father hung up the telephone and dropped into an old easy chair, observing Carmen from there. "Now no one's gone to work today, hopefully it's nothing serious," he said. The mother was clattering in the kitchen, as though she were stumbling at every turn. The sun came in through the window from the garden, but it lent no warmth or cheer to that room in which everything had come to a standstill. Their thoughts and suspicions lay hidden or veiled by fear. Their anxiety and distress were shielded by a desolate silence.

The boy looked at his watch.

"It's almost nine," he said, just to say something.

"The doctor's on his way—luckily he was still at home," said the father.

"The Last Time I Saw Paris" began to play as the musical clock struck nine—it was the clock they'd given to the mother on her last birthday. She came out of the kitchen with a steaming cup of tea, her eyes red.

"Go on upstairs," her husband said to her. "We'll bring her up."

"Let's go upstairs, Carmen."

Father and brother lifted her to her feet. She offered no resistance to being led, and slowly began to climb the stairs. She was very distant from herself and from that moment. Her eyes gazed fixedly toward some other place, some other time. She resembled a ghostly figure drifting between rocks. They didn't make it to the top of the stairs. A pounding on the door to the street halted them. The brother ran downstairs, thinking it was the doctor. He opened the door and the police barged in.

The Last Summer

SHE WORE A chiffon dress with flounces at the neck and sleeves; her dark chestnut hair, pulled back with a black velvet bow, revealed a young face with harmonious features, the most striking of which were her eyes, shadowed by long lashes. She radiated not only the freshness of youth, but also great peace and happiness. But that beautiful girl—for she truly was beautiful—so well groomed and exhaling calm from every pore, was inside a picture frame, placed on top of the dresser, by the mirror. That was how she'd looked at eighteen, before her marriage. Pepe had wanted a portrait of her for his birthday; it had come out very well, it really had, and she felt an immense grief as she compared the young woman in the photograph to the image reflected in the mirror, her own image: that of a mature, thickset woman with a weary face, who was showing signs of aging and neglect, or rather of letting herself go completely: hair dull and streaked with gray, wearing low-heeled shoes and a tired old dress no longer in fashion. No one would think that the girl gazing at her from inside the photograph had once been she, yes, she, so full of dreams and projects, whereas now ... "What's wrong, Mamá?" Ricardo asked her, because she was sitting with her face buried in her hands in front of the dresser, where she had gone to fix herself up a little before going out. Dispirited, she changed her clothing and got herself ready. "Of course it's impossible to be lively and happy when you know all too well that you're no longer a woman but a shadow, a shadow that will fade away slowly, slowly ..." She covered her mouth with her handkerchief to stifle a sob—lately she had been feeling oversensitive and depressed, and she cried easily.

It was the beginning of summer, a dry and suffocating summer, when she had begun to feel unwell: sometimes it was an intense nausea in the morning and waves of heat that rose to her head, or powerful dizzy spells, as if the whole room and the furniture were spinning—dizzy spells that sometimes persisted all day. She had lost her appetite too—nothing appealed to her and she found everything disgusting, and if it were up to her she would have gone days without eating, having only a coffee or some juice. An immense fatigue had begun to take hold of her, making it impossible for her to complete her daily chores—she who had always worked from morning to night, like a slave. Everything she did now took enormous effort, an effort that grew greater each day. "It must be my age." An age that most women so dread, and that she in particular saw approaching as if it were the end of everything: sterility, old age, serenity, death ... The days passed and her condition became so unbearable that she decided to go see the doctor. Maybe he could give her something to make this difficult stage less onerous.

After examining her carefully, the doctor gave her an affectionate pat on the shoulder and congratulated her. She was going to be a mother again. She couldn't believe her ears. "I never would've believed it—at my age, I thought it was ... I mean, that they were symptoms of ... but how is it possible, Doctor?" And she had to ask him several times if he was absolutely certain of the diagnosis, since it was very unusual for this to happen at her age. "That's what it is, my dear, and nothing more, follow my instructions and come see me in a month, don't worry, if you take care of yourself everything will be fine, you'll see, I'll expect to see you again in a month." He prescribed her some medicines. And she, who for days and days, and even just a few hours before, had wept at merely thinking she had arrived at that terrible age when motherhood, freshness, and vigor had come to an end, now, on receiving the news, experienced no happiness; on the contrary, she felt a great confusion and fatigue. Because, of course, it was a real burden to have another child after seven years, when you've already had six others and you're not twenty years old anymore, when you have no one at all to help you, and you have to do everything in the house and manage it all with hardly any money, and with prices going up all the time. Those were her thoughts as she rode the bus home: watching the streets pass by, she thought they looked as sad as the afternoon, as sad as she was. Because she didn't want to start all over again: back to the bottles every three hours, washing diapers all day, spending the nights awake, when all she wanted was to sleep and sleep—no, it couldn't be, she no longer had the strength or the patience to take care of another child, it was already enough to deal with six of them and with Pepe, so curt with her, so indifferent—"He's no match for you, *hija*, he'll never achieve anything in life, he has no aspirations, the only thing he'll do is give you a bunch of kids"—yes, one more child, and he wouldn't make the slightest effort to find another job and earn more, what did he care if she had to work miracles with their expenses, or if she died of fatigue.

That night she gave him the news. The children had already gone to bed and they were in the living room watching television like they always did after dinner. Pepe slipped an arm around her shoulders and grazed her cheek with a kiss. "Every child brings his own food and clothing, don't worry, we'll come out ahead like we always have." And she sat there gazing at the television, where something senseless was moving, while inside her a world of thoughts and feelings swarmed. The days and weeks passed, and she still couldn't find a sense of resignation or hope. Her fatigue increased as the days went by, and an intense weakness obliged her to lie down, sometimes several times throughout the day. And so the summer passed.

At night, between dreams, Pepe would hear her crying or feel her shaking, but he barely noticed her sleeplessness. Naturally Pepe would sleep like a log! He didn't have to give birth to another child, or take care of it. "Children are a reward, a gift." But for a forty-five-year-old woman with six children, who no longer has the strength and energy to keep going, another child isn't a reward at all—it's a punishment.

Sometimes she got up in the middle of the night and sat by the window. There, in the dark, she heard the crickets in the little garden below, where she grew fruits and vegetables, and dawn would surprise her with her eyes still open and her hands clenched in anguish.

She went to see the doctor at the end of the month, and again the following one. He adjusted her prescriptions a little, but his recommendation was always the same: "Try not to tire yourself out so much, my dear, get more rest, relax." She would return home, walking heavily.

On one of those nights when she couldn't manage to sleep, when the heat and desperation forced her to get up and walk around, she went outside to refresh herself a little and leaned against the railing of the stairs that descended from the bedrooms down to the garden. She breathed the perfumed odor of the night-blooming jasmine that she usually loved so much, but now it seemed too intense and it revolted her. She was observing the fireflies with indifference as they lit up and went out, populating the night with little flashes of light, when something warm and gelatinous began to run from between her legs. She looked down and on the floor saw a bouquet of plucked poppies. She felt her forehead bathed in cold sweat and her legs giving out beneath her. She steadied herself on the railing while shouting for her husband. Pepe carried her to bed and ran for the doctor. "I told you again and again that you should rest, my dear, that you shouldn't wear yourself out so much," said the doctor as he finished examining her, giving her a quick pat on the shoulder. "Try to sleep, tomorrow I'll come see you." Before falling asleep, she asked Pepe to wrap up the coagula in some newspaper and bury it all in a corner of the garden, so the children wouldn't see it.

The sun was flooding her room when she awoke. She'd slept for many hours. Her children had gone to school without making any noise. Pepe brought her a cup of *café con leche* and a sweet roll that she ate with pleasure. She was hungry. And when Pepe went out to ask his sister to come stay for a few days while she recuperated, she lay there thinking, and couldn't help but feel a great sense of relief that she'd escaped from that awful nightmare. Of course it was painful that it had happened in such a sad and disagreeable way, but things don't happen the way we imagine they will—they happen the way they must. Of course she hadn't wanted another child now, no, it would have been too much for her— but not like this, she wished it hadn't happened this way, it upset her terribly, and she began to weep disconsolately for a long while, until she fell asleep once more.

Within a few days everything had returned to normal and she was performing her housework as always. Taking care not to tire herself out too much, she managed to keep busy all day, so that she wouldn't have time to sit down and dwell on things or be invaded by remorse. She tried to put it all behind her, to forget that devastating summer that had finally come to an end, and she had almost managed to do so, until that day when she asked Pepito to cut a few tomatoes from the garden. "No, Mami, the worms are there too."

Her ears began to ring, the furniture and everything in the room spun around her; her vision clouded and she had to sit down so as not to fall. She was soaked in sweat and consumed by anguish. Surely Pepe, clumsy as ever, hadn't dug deep enough and then ... but how horrifying, the maggots crawling out, crawling out ...

That day there was hardly anything to eat, and what she did manage to prepare was either too salty or half-raw or burnt, because she had begun to spin inside a whirlwind of ideas and maddening fears.

Her whole life changed all at once. She did her chores nervously, wracked with anxiety; she made the beds carelessly, gave a few sweeps with the broom, and ran to peer through the windows that overlooked the garden; she would start to dust the furniture, and go again to the window; she forgot what she was doing, she left puddles on the floor when she mopped, things fell from her hands, she would break dishes, then pick up the pieces in a hurry and throw them in the trash can so that nobody would see them and suspect her; she spent long hours leaning on the railing, watching, watching ...

She hardly spoke to Pepe and the children. Everything bothered her: if they asked her something, if they chatted with her, if they made noise, if they turned on the radio, if they played, if they shouted, if they watched television ... She wanted to be alone, to think, to observe ... she didn't want to be distracted, she needed to be alert, listening, watching, listening, watching ...

That afternoon, Pepe had gone downtown to get a haircut and buy new shoes. The three littlest ones went to Catechism like every Saturday, and the older ones were playing basketball. She was alone in the modest living room, trying uselessly to mend socks and patch shirts and pants, as she used to be able to do quite ably and quickly while watching *Saturdays with Saldaña*, which she loved, above all *Nostalgia* ... but that was no longer possible, nothing interested her anymore but listening, watching, staying alert, watching, listening ... At nearly six in the evening she heard a light rasping sound, something dragging itself across the floor, barely touching the surface; she sat still, without breathing ... yes, there wasn't the slightest doubt, that's what it was, they were coming closer, closer, slowly and steadily ... and her eyes perceived a faint shadow beneath the door ... yes, they were there, they had arrived; there was no more time to lose—soon she would be at their mercy ... She ran toward the table that held the old porcelain oil lamp, an heirloom from her mother. With trembling hands she unscrewed the oil tank and doused herself with its contents from head to toe until she was completely soaked; then, with what was left, she sprinkled a circumference, a little circle, around herself. Just before she lit the match she managed to see them, struggling their way through the crack in the door ... but she was more clever and had beat them at their game. Nothing would be left for them to avenge themselves upon but a pile of smoldering ashes.

The Funeral

for Julio and Aurora Cortázar

HE AWOKE IN a hospital, in a small room where everything was white and spotlessly clean, among oxygen tanks and bags of intravenous fluid, unable to move or speak, no visitors allowed. With consciousness, there also came the desperation of realizing he was in a hospital, and under such strict conditions. All his attempts to communicate with his office, to see his secretary, were useless. The doctors and nurses begged him to rest and forget everything for a while, not to worry about a thing. "Your health is what's most important, get some rest, relax, relax, try to sleep, don't think so much ..." But how could he stop thinking about his office, abandoned suddenly, without instructions, without oversight? How could he not worry about work and all the business he'd left unfinished? He had put off so many things to take care of until the next day. And poor Raquel, who didn't know a thing ... His wife and sons kept him company silently. They took turns at his bedside but didn't let him speak or move. "Everything's fine at the office, don't worry, rest easy." He closed his eyes and pretended to sleep, mentally gave orders to his secretary, reviewed all his affairs, sank into despair. For the first time in his life he felt handcuffed, utterly dependent on the will of others, unable to rebel because he knew it was useless to try. He wondered too how his friends had taken the news of his illness, what kind of comments they might have made. Occasionally, a bit drowsy from thinking and thinking, he mistook the sound of the oxygen machine for his voice recorder, and it seemed to him then that he was at the office dictating as he usually did when he arrived in the mornings; he dictated at length until, suddenly and without knocking on the door, his secretary came in with an enormous syringe and pricked him cruelly; then finally he opened his eyes and found himself back in his hospital room.

Everything had begun in such a simple way that he hadn't given it much importance. He'd attributed that tiny, persistent pain in his right arm merely to rheumatism caused by the constant humidity, to sedentary living, perhaps over-indulgence in drinking ... perhaps. Suddenly he felt that something inside him was breaking, or opening, that he was exploding, and an agonizing pain, red, like a blade of fire piercing through him; then the fall, without crying out, falling deeper and deeper, blacker and blacker, deeper and blacker, endless, airless, in the claws of mute asphyxiation.

After some time, almost a month later, they allowed him to go home, where he divided his time between sitting in a reclining chair and lying in bed. Eternal days spent doing nothing, reading only the newspaper—and that only after he forcefully insisted on it. Counting the hours, the minutes, waiting for morning to end and afternoon to come, then nighttime, another day, another, and so on ... Waiting with genuine anxiety for some friend to come and chat for a little while. Almost daily he asked the doctors, with marked impatience, when he would be better, when he could resume his ordinary life. "We're doing well, wait a little longer ..." or "Be calm, these things are very serious and they can't be fixed as fast as one might like. Help us out ..." And that's how it always was. He'd never thought such a thing could happen to him, he who had always been such a healthy man, so full of activity—that he would suddenly have to interrupt the rhythm of his life and find himself trapped in a reclining chair, there in his house. For years he had hardly spent time there, except to sleep, arriving nearly always after midnight, or maybe eating a meal there once in a while (on his sons' birthdays and a few Sundays he spent with them). These days he spoke with his wife only when strictly necessary, about matters having to do with the boys, which they needed to discuss or to agree upon, or when they had some social commitment, to attend a party or to entertain at home. The distance between them had arisen just a few years after their marriage. He couldn't tie himself down to one woman—he was too restless, maybe too dissatisfied. She hadn't understood. Reproofs, unpleasant scenes, long faces ... until he finally ended up disregarding her completely and arranging his life as he pleased. There was no divorce; his wife wouldn't accept such an anti-Catholic solution, and they settled on merely being parents to their children and keeping up appearances. She had grown so estranged from him that he no longer knew what to talk about with her or what to say to her. Now she tended to him with marked solicitude, and he couldn't understand if it was out of some remaining trace of affection, her sense of duty, or maybe pity at seeing him so sick. Whatever her reasons, he found himself uncomfortable in front of her, though not because he felt any kind of regret (he'd never felt regret in his life)—only his own self had validity, others functioned in relation to his desires.

Few friends visited him. The closest ones: "How do you feel?"—"How're your spirits?"—"You look great today"—"Gotta pluck up your courage, cheer up"—"You'll be better any day now" — "Look at that healthy face, you don't look sick at all." At this he felt the uncontrollable desire to shout that it wasn't his face that was sick, how could they be such idiots — but he controlled himself, they surely said it in good faith, plus it wasn't fair to be rude to the people who had come to chat with him for a while. Those moments with his friends, and the time he spent with his sons when they weren't at school, were his only distractions.

Every day he waited for the moment when his wife took a shower; then he would pick up the telephone and, in a very low voice, speak with Raquel. Sometimes she answered at the first ring; other times she took longer, picking up after several rings; other times she didn't answer at all, and then he imagined things that tortured him terribly: he saw her in bed, in total abandon, in someone else's company still, not even hearing the telephone ring, having already forgotten him and all the promises she'd made to him … In those moments he wanted to hurl away the telephone, toss aside the blankets that warmed his legs, and run, arriving there suddenly, surprising her (women were all the same: lying, false, treacherous, "the hole for the dead, the living to the bread," wretched, sellouts, cynical, not worth a damn, but no one made a mockery out of him, he'd put her in her place, he'd throw her out in the street where she belonged, he'd teach her how to behave, to be decent, he'd find himself another girl and rub it in her face, that Raquel would see, she'd see …). Pale as a dead man and trembling all over, he'd shout for a bit of water and a tranquilizer. Another day she would answer the telephone right away and he'd forget everything.

The days passed with no improvement. "Be patient, these things take time, we've already told you that, wait a little longer." But he began to notice fairly evident things: the

doses of medicine being reduced or becoming mere seda-
tives; very few X-rays, fewer electrocardiograms; the doctors' visits growing ever shorter and without comment; the
permission to see his secretary and deal with the most urgent
business with her; the noticeable worry that appeared on the
faces of his wife and sons; the exaggerated solicitude they
showed by hardly wanting to leave him alone, their gazes
filled with tenderness ... For several days his wife had left
the door open between their adjoining bedrooms, and several times during the night she would walk between them
with the pretext of seeing if he needed anything. One night
when he wasn't sleeping he heard her sobbing. He had no
more doubts then, nor did he harbor any further hopes. He
understood everything at once: there was nothing to be done
and the end was perhaps near. Again he felt as though he
were being torn apart, deeper still than what he'd felt during his attack. The limitless, hopeless pain of the man who
suddenly hears his sentence and has nothing to await now
but death, of the man who has to leave it all behind when
he least expected it, when everything was organized for life,
for physical and economic well-being, when he had managed to lay the foundations of an enviable situation, when he
had three intelligent and handsome sons who were about to
become men, when he had found a girl like Raquel. Death
had never been in his plans or his thoughts. Not even when
some friend or relative died had he thought about his own
disappearance—he felt full of life and energy. He had so
many projects, so many deals planned, he wanted so many
things! He ardently desired, with all his soul, to find himself in some other day, sitting at his desk dictating into the
recorder, running here and there, running to beat time. If
only it were all an awful nightmare! But the cruelest part was
that he couldn't lie to himself. With each passing day he had

observed that his body was growing less and less responsive, that his fatigue had become overwhelming, his breathing more labored.

This discovery plunged him into a deep depression. He spent several days this way, not speaking, not wanting to know about his business, caring about nothing. Then, almost without realizing it, he began, after so much thinking and thinking about death, to grow familiar with it, to adapt to the idea. There were times when he almost felt lucky to know his end was near, that it hadn't happened to him the way it did to those poor people who die all of a sudden and don't even give you the time to say "Jesus help you"; those who die in their sleep and pass from one dream to another, leaving everything in disarray. It was preferable to know it, preferable to prepare things himself, make his will correctly, and also—why not?—make the arrangements for the funeral. He wanted to be buried, first of all, the way a man who had worked all his life to attain a respectable social and economic position deserved, and secondly, according to his own tastes and not the tastes and convenience of the rest. "It's all the same now, why so much ostentation? Those are vanities that mean nothing now"—that's what dead people's relatives tended to say. But for the person who was leaving it all behind, it did mean something for these last few formalities to be carried out according to his wishes. He began by thinking about which cemetery would be best. The English cemetery was renowned as the most distinguished, and that would make it the most costly. He'd been there before, to bury two friends, and he didn't find it bad, or depressing; it seemed more like a park, with many statues and well-groomed lawns. Nevertheless it emanated a certain established chill: everything symmetrical, orderly, exact, like the English mentality, and to be honest with himself, he had never liked the English, with their eternal mask of serenity, so methodical, so punctual, so full of periods and commas. He'd always had a hard time understanding them when he'd had to do business with them; they were meticulous, sticklers for detail, and such good bankers that they annoyed him profoundly. He who was so decisive in everything, who often played his business deals purely on a hunch, who upon making a decision had given his final word, who closed one deal and went straight to the next—he couldn't stand those types who circled back to the beginning of the matter, made a thousand observations, established clauses, imposed a thousand conditions. What a pain! ... He'd do better to think about another cemetery. Then he remembered the Jardín, where his aunt Matilde was buried. There was no doubt that it was the prettiest: outside the city, on the mountainside, full of light, air, sun (incidentally, he'd never found out how his aunt's monument turned out; he had no time for such things, not for lack of interest, of course! His wife had told him it came out quite well). Pepe Antúñez was there too— such a good friend, and what a drinker! He never folded, he held out until the end. When he was in high spirits, he liked to listen to Guty Cárdenas songs, and no matter how much they told him to lay off the bottle he never paid attention. "If it weren't for this," he'd say, lifting his glass, "and one or two other things, life would be so boring!" And he died of it. But he hadn't been too shabby a drinker himself: a few whiskeys to whet his appetite, a bottle of wine with dinner, then some cognac or a cream liqueur, and if he hadn't been so busy with work all the time he might have ended up like poor Pepe ... He also thought about the French Cemetery. "It has class, no doubt about that, but it's the one that looks the most like a cemetery, so austere, so depressing. Strange that it's like that, since the French always seem so full of life and good cheer ... especially the women ... Renée, Denise, Viviàne ..." And he smiled in satisfaction: "Pretty girls!" When he was around forty he had thought having a French lover was very stylish—and it provoked a certain envy among one's friends, since people believe that French and Italian women know all the mysteries of the bedroom. Later, with age and experience, he learned that erotic ardor and wisdom aren't national traits but entirely personal ones. He'd had two French lovers back then. Viviàne was nothing serious. He had been introduced to Renée at a cocktail party hosted by the French Embassy:

"I just arrived ... I'm very disoriented ... I don't know how to begin my studies, you know how it is, such a foreign country ..."

"What you need is a godfather to give you some orientation, something like a tutor ..."

The look with which she accepted the offer was so loaded with meaning that he knew he could aspire to be something more than a tutor. And so it was—without preamble, without beating around the bush, they became involved. As naturally as other women took a bath or brushed their teeth, those girls went to bed. He had given her a small but pleasant and cozy apartment: a little studio with a bar, a kitchenette, and a bathroom. In the studio there was a red velvet couch that served as seat and bed, a table, and two bookshelves. Renée brought only a few books, a typewriter, and her personal items. He gave her a record player so she could listen to music while she studied. She never cooked in the apartment, saying she didn't have time, she was taking so many classes, and she always complained that she ate poorly, in any old cheap place. Her siblings were still in school; her father, a lawyer who was old already, didn't practice much. They sent her barely anything for her expenses. He couldn't stand seeing Renée live that way, and he gave her a Diners Club card so she could eat in nice restaurants. Before long he had to exchange her apartment for a larger and, of course, more costly one. She constantly complained that the apartment was too cramped, that she felt herself asphyxiating, that her neighbors made a lot of noise and kept her from working ... Then he had to buy her an automobile, because she wasted lots of time going to and from school, the buses were always full of filthy people and uncouth louts who besieged her with impertinent remarks, sometimes to the point that she needed to ask someone for help—and of course he couldn't allow that! He had been very attracted to Renée, but he never became passionate about her. The relationship lasted about a year. Then at one point she stopped letting him see her so often: "I have a lot of studying to do, I failed a class, and I want to pass the proficiency exam, a classmate said he would help me with it ..." When she had to study, which was almost every night, he would stop by to bring her a box of chocolates or some snacks; she would open the door and accept the gift but wouldn't let him come in: "With you here, I won't be able to study, and I have to pass the exam." She'd give him a quick kiss and close the door with an *au revoir, chéri*. A little annoyed, he'd go off in search of a friend to see a show with, or have a few drinks before going to sleep at his house ... That day he brought her the chocolates as usual. They had said goodbye and he was already leaving, when he noticed that his shoelace was untied, and he crouched down to tie it, right next to the apartment door. That was when he heard their laughter and a few remarks: "Look, he brought us our chocolates." "Poor old fool!" said the boy. Then more laughter, and then ... What he'd felt! All the blood rushed suddenly to his head, he wanted to fling open the door and surprise them, dish out blows, bellow in rage; and he wasn't in love, it was his pride, his vanity, that had been injured for the first time. That little French girl had really played him! He lit a cigarette and inhaled a few puffs. It wasn't worth it, he reflected suddenly, he would only end up looking ridiculous, or maybe he'd go too far and kill the boy, and what then? What a scandal that would be for the newspapers! A man of his position cuckolded by an undergraduate, what a laugh! His friends would mock him for the rest of his life, he could imagine it already. In addition, his whole family would find out, the clients who considered him such a serious and honorable person ... No, in no way would he compromise himself with a matter of this sort. He took the elevator, left the building, parked his car a short distance away, and waited, smoking cigarette after cigarette. He wanted to know what time the boy would leave, to be completely sure. He waited until seven in the morning, when he saw him walk out smoothing back his hair, yawning ... After that she'd come looking for him many times—she called him at his office, waited for him at the entrance, sought him out in their usual bars. He remained unapproachable; she no longer interested him: there were thousands like her, or better. Denise didn't mean anything, he slept with her two or three times, and that was plenty. All of his friends and almost half the city had passed through her bed at least once; she was extremely boring and obsessed with marrying whoever would have her, plus she was long and scrawny, she didn't have anything ...

He decided finally on the Jardín Cemetery; he would lie near his aunt Matilde. After all, she was like his second mother, she had taken him in when he was left an orphan and had given him love and protection. He would order them to place an elegant and understated marker on his grave: a marble tombstone with his name and the date. He would buy a plot for the entire family and have them bring Aunt Matilde and his brothers there. Buying a plot had its advantages: it was a solid investment, since land always goes up in price, even in cemeteries; it also ensured that his sons and wife would have somewhere to be buried; it wouldn't be at all difficult for them to run through the inheritance he was going to leave them with—he'd seen so many cases of generous inheritances painfully squandered! His coffin would be metal, big and durable; he didn't want to repeat what had happened to Pancho Rocha: when he went to the wake, he had the unpleasant impression that they had put Pancho in a box that was too small for him. He would ask for the most elegant and expensive hearse so that the people who saw his funeral procession passing by would think: *That must have been someone very important and very rich*. As for the funeral parlor where they would hold the wake, that was no problem—Gayosso was the best of them all. These arrangements would be included in the will he had decided to give to his lawyer, which would be opened as soon as he died, giving his family time to observe his last wishes.

The days began to seem shorter. With so much thinking and thinking, the hours flew by unnoticed. He no longer suffered waiting for his friends' visits; on the contrary, he wished that they wouldn't interrupt him, and that his secretary wouldn't drop by with a report or consult him about his business. His family began to speculate about what might have caused this change in him after so many days sunk in dejection. He was visibly excited by his plans; his eyes sparkled as before. True, he stayed silent, but he was occupied with something very important. They began to think he must be planning one of those big business deals he was always making. This change was a relief for his family: his depression had made the sentence hanging over his head even harder on them.

He began by writing his will; he would leave his funeral arrangements for last, now that they were completely planned and decided. His fortune—property, stocks, cash—would be divided equally between his wife and his three sons; his wife would remain executor until the boys had finished with school and were ready to begin working. To Raquel he would leave the house he had given her and enough money to start a business of some kind. To his sister, Sofía, some shares of petroleum stock—the poor woman was always strapped for cash, with so many children and with Emilio, who was terrible at business and was always losing money. To his secretary he would give the house in Colonia del Valle: she had been so patient with him, so faithful and obliging, she had worked for him for almost fifteen years ... His brother, Pascual, didn't need anything, being just as rich as he was. But his aunt Carmen did, although it was true that he'd never felt much affection for that old neurasthenic who was always scolding and criticizing him; still, that's just how she was, and she was already so old that she couldn't have many years left, so she might as well have whatever she desired.

It took him several days to write the will. He didn't want anyone to find out about its contents until the time was right. He wrote during the brief moments when they left him alone. When someone came, he would hide the papers in his desk and lock the drawer. Everything had been laid out with perfect clarity, so as not to allow for confusion or disputes; it was a well-organized and very fair will, nobody would be cheated by it. All that was left were the arrangements for his funeral, which he would add as soon as he had a chance.

There were two things he wished before dying: to go out

into the street one last time, walking on his own, with no one watching and without anyone in his house knowing about it, to move about like one of those poor people who stroll along in peace without knowing that their own death is already by their side, and that when they cross the street a car will run them over and kill them, or those who die reading the newspaper while waiting in line for the bus; and he also wanted to see Raquel once more—he had missed her so much! The last time they were together they had dined outside the city; the restaurant was intimate and pleasant, very low lighting, the music subdued, slow ... After three drinks Raquel wanted to dance; he had refused: it seemed ridiculous at his age, he might see someone he knew, dancing wasn't for him anymore; but she insisted and insisted until he could no longer refuse. He still remembered the contact of her so amply endowed body, her clean scent of a young woman; and as if feeling a premonition, he had drawn her closer to him.

When he dropped her off at her house, he didn't stay with her; he wasn't feeling well, he had an unfamiliar feeling of anxiety, something strange that oppressed his chest, suffocated him and made breathing difficult. He had barely managed to reach his house and open the garage ... He would fulfill these wishes without telling anyone beforehand; he would escape. It would be easy to do after the afternoon meal: his wife always took a short nap and the servants always stayed to chat around the table long after they finished eating. He always spent his afternoons in the library, which had a door that opened onto the garage; he would slip through it without being seen. In the library's closet he kept a coat and a rain jacket ... When he returned he would explain everything—they would understand. In his situation nothing could harm him anymore, his death was irremediable. Sitting still like a log or going out for a stroll, it was all the same at this point ... At that moment his wife came in: the afternoon was cold, it was drizzling, it would be best for him to go to bed. He willingly agreed and let himself be led there. Before falling asleep he thought again with great joy that tomorrow he would make his last excursion outside. He felt as excited as a boy sneaking out of the house for a night on the town: he would see Raquel, he would see the streets again, he would walk through them ...

He was in the library, as usual, sitting in his eternal reclining chair. He didn't hear the slightest sound; there didn't seem to be a soul in the entire house. He smiled, satisfied: everything would be even easier than he'd expected. It was nearly four o'clock when he decided to go out. From the closet he took the rain jacket, a wool scarf, and a hat. He bundled up properly and pressed his ear to the door, but there wasn't the least sign of life in the house—everything was silent. He calmly left through the garage door, not without first donning a pair of dark sunglasses so he could pass through the streets unrecognized. He wanted to walk alone. The afternoon was gray and chilly, an autumn afternoon turning to winter. He adjusted his scarf and turned up the collar of the jacket; he hastened from the house as quickly as possible. Then, confident, he slackened his pace and stopped to buy cigarettes. He lit one and savored it with delight: it had been so long since he'd smoked! At first he'd asked his friends to bring him cigarettes; they never did, and eventually he stopped asking. He walked aimlessly for a while, until he realized that he was slowly heading in the opposite direction from Raquel's house; he changed his path. Arriving at a corner, he stopped: a funeral procession was coming and he didn't have time to cross the street in front of it. He would wait ... First, several buses full of people dressed in mourning passed by;

they were followed by a black hearse, nothing ostentatious, a common, everyday one without flourishes: "It must be a modest funeral." Nevertheless, behind the hearse, several trucks went by bearing large floral offerings, huge and expensive wreaths: "Then it must have been someone important." Then came the family members' automobile, a black Cadillac of the latest model, "just like mine." When the car passed, he could make out inside it the pale and grief-torn faces of his sons and of his wife who, wracked with sobs, covered her mouth with a handkerchief so as not to cry out.